THE WORKS OF ANATOLE FRANCE
IN AN ENGLISH TRANSLATION
EDITED BY FREDERIC CHAPMAN

THE ELM-TREE ON THE MALL

THE ELM-TREE ON THE MALL

A CHRONICLE OF OUR OWN TIMES

BY ANATOLE FRANCE

A TRANSLATION BY
M. P. WILLCOCKS

WILDSIDE PRESS

Published by
Wildside Press, LLC
P.O. Box 301
Holicong, PA 18928-0301 USA
www.wildsidepress.com

Wildside Press Edition: MMIII

THE ELM-TREE ON THE MALL

THE ELM-TREE ON THE MALL

HE salon which the Cardinal-Archbishop used as a reception room had been fitted, in the time of Louis XV., with panellings of carved wood painted a light grey. Seated figures of women surrounded by trophies filled the angles of the cornices. The mirror on the chimney-piece being in two divisions, was covered, as to its lower half, with a drapery of crimson velvet which threw into relief a pure white statue of Our Lady of Lourdes with her pretty blue scarf. Along the walls, in the middle of the panels, hung enamel plates framed in reddish plush, portraits of Popes Pius IX. and Leo XIII. printed in colours, and pieces of embroidery, either souvenirs of Rome or gifts from the pious ladies of the diocese. The gilded side-tables were loaded with plaster models of Gothic or Romanesque churches : the Cardinal-Archbishop was fond of buildings. From the plaster rose hung a Merovingian chandelier executed from the designs of M. Quatrebarbe, diocesan architect and Knight of the Order of Saint Gregory.

Tucking his cassock up above his violet stockings and warming his short, stout legs at the fire, Monseigneur was dictating a pastoral letter, whilst, seated at a large table of brass and tortoiseshell, on which stood an ivory crucifix, the vicar-general, M. de Goulet, was writing : *So that nothing may occur to sadden for us the joys of our retreat.* . . .

Monseigneur dictated in a dry, colourless voice. He was a very short man, but the great head with its square face softened by age was carried erect. Notwithstanding its coarse and homely lineaments, his face was expressive of subtlety and a kind of dignity born of habit and the love of command.

" *The joys of our retreat.* . . . Here you will expound the ideas of harmony, of the subduing of the mind, of that submission to the powers that be which is so necessary, and which I have already dealt with in my previous pastoral letters."

M. de Goulet raised his long, pale, refined head adorned by beautiful curled locks as though by a Louis Quatorze wig.

" But this time," said he, " would it not be expedient, while repeating these declarations, to show that reserve appropriate to the position of the secular powers, shaken as they are by internal convulsions and henceforth incapable of imparting to their covenants what they themselves do not possess—I mean continuity and stability? For you must see, Monseigneur, that the decline of parliamentary predominance . . ."

The Cardinal-Archbishop shook his head.

" Without reservation, Monsieur de Goulet, without any species of reservation. You are full of learning and piety, Monsieur de Goulet, but your old pastor can still give you a few lessons in discretion, before handing over the government of the diocese, at his death, to your youthful energy. Have we not to congratulate ourselves upon the attitude of M. *le préfet* Worms-Clavelin, who regards our schools and our labours with favour ? And are we not welcoming to our table to-morrow the general in command of the division and the president-in-chief ? And, *à propos* of that, let me see the menu."

The Cardinal-Archbishop inspected it, made alterations and additions, and gave special directions that the game should be ordered from Rivoire, the poacher to the prefecture.

A servant entered and presented him with a card on a silver tray.

Having read the name of Abbé Lantaigne, head of the high seminary, on the card, Monseigneur turned towards his vicar-general.

"I'll wager," said he, "that M. Lantaigne is coming to complain to me again about M. Guitrel."

Abbé de Goulet rose to leave the salon. But Monseigneur stopped him.

"Stay! I want you to share with me the pleasure of listening to M. Lantaigne, who, as you know, is spoken of as the finest preacher in the diocese. For, if one listened only to public opinion, it would seem that he preaches better than you, dear Monsieur de Goulet. But that is not my opinion. Between ourselves, I care neither for his inflated style nor for his involved scholarship. He is terribly wearisome, and I am keeping you here to help me to get rid of him as quickly as possible."

A priest entered the salon and bowed. He was very tall and immensely corpulent, with a serious, simple, abstracted face.

At sight of him Monseigneur exclaimed gaily :

"Ah! good-day, Monsieur l'abbé Lantaigne. At the very moment that you sent in your name the vicar-general and I were talking about you. We were saying that you are the most distinguished orator in the diocese, and that the Lenten course you preached at Saint-Exupère is proof positive of your great talents and profound scholarship."

Abbé Lantaigne reddened. He was sensitive to praise, and it was by the door of pride alone that the Enemy could find entrance to his soul.

"Monseigneur," he answered, his face lit up by a smile which quickly died away, "the approval of Your Eminence gives me a deep delight which comes felicitously to soothe the opening of an interview which is a painful one to me. For it is a complaint which the head of the high seminary has the misfortune to pour into your paternal ears."

Monseigneur interrupted him :

"Tell me, Monsieur Lantaigne, has that Lenten course at Saint-Exupère been printed ?"

"A synopsis of it appeared in the diocesan *Semaine religieuse.* I am moved, Monseigneur, by the marks of interest which you deign to show in my apostolic labours. Alas ! it is long enough ago since I first entered the pulpit. In 1880, when I had too many sermons, I gave them to M. Roquette, who has since been raised to a bishopric."

"Ah !" cried Monseigneur, with a smile, "that good M. Roquette ! When I went last year *ad limina apostolorum* I met M. Roquette for the first time just as he was gaily setting out for the Vatican. A week later I met him in Saint-Peter's, where he was imbibing the solace that he much needed after being refused the cardinal's hat."

"And why," demanded M. Lantaigne, in a voice that whistled like a whip-lash, "why should the purple have descended on the shoulders of this poor creature, a mediocrity in character, a nonentity in doctrine, whose mental density has made him ridiculous, and whose sole recommendation is that he has sat at table with the President of the Republic at a masonic banquet ?   Could M. Roquette only rise above himself, he would be astonished at finding himself a bishop.   In these times of trial, when a future confronts us pregnant with awful menace as well as with gracious promise, it would be expedient to build up a body of clergy powerful both in character and in scholarship.   And in fact, Monseigneur, I come to interview Your Eminence about another Roquette, about another priest who is unfitted to sustain the weight of his great duties.   The professor of rhetoric at the high seminary, M. l'abbé Guitrel . . ."

Monseigneur interrupted with a feigned jest, and asked, with a laugh, whether Abbé Guitrel were in a fair way to become a bishop in his turn.

" What an idea, Monseigneur !" cried Abbé Lantaigne.   "If perchance this man were raised to a bishopric, we should behold once more the days of Cautinus, when an unworthy pontiff defiled the see of Saint Martin."

The Cardinal-Archbishop, curled up in his armchair, remarked genially :

" Cautinus, Bishop Cautinus " (it was the first time he had heard the name), " Cautinus who was a successor of Saint Martin. Are you quite sure that

this Cautinus behaved as badly as they make out ?
It is an interesting point in the history of the Gallic
Church concerning which I should much like to
have the opinion of so learned a man as yourself,
Monsieur Lantaigne."

The head of the high seminary drew himself up.

"The testimony, Monseigneur, of Gregory of
Tours is explicit in the passage touching Bishop
Cautinus. This successor of the blessed Martin
lived in such luxury and robbed the Church of its
treasures to such an extent that, at the end of two
years of his administration, all the sacred vessels were
in the hands of the Jews of Tours. And if I have
coupled the name of Cautinus with that of this unhappy M. Guitrel, it is not without reason. M.
Guitrel carries off the artistic curios, wood-carvings,
or finely chased vessels, which are still to be found
in country churches, in the care of ignorant churchwardens, and it is for the benefit of the Jews that he
devotes himself to this robbery."

"For the benefit of the Jews?" demanded
Monseigneur. "What is this that you are telling
me?"

"For the benefit of the Jews," returned Abbé
Lantaigne, "and to embellish the drawing-rooms of
M. *le préfet* Worms-Clavelin, Jew and freemason.
Madame Worms-Clavelin is fond of antiquities.
Through the medium of M. Guitrel she has gained

possession of the copes treasured for three hundred years in the vestry of the church at Lusancy, and she has, I am told, turned them into seats of the kind called *poufs*."

Monseigneur shook his head.

"*Poufs !* But if the transfer or these disused vestments has been conducted legally, I do not see that Bishop Cautinus . . . I mean M. Guitrel, has done wrong in taking part in this lawful transaction. There is no reason why these copes of the pious priests of Lusancy should be revered as relics of the saints.   There is no sacrilege in selling their cast-off clothes to be turned into *poufs*."

M. de Goulet, who had been nibbling his pen for some moments, could not refrain from a murmur. He deplored the fact that the churches should be thus robbed of their artistic treasures by infidels. The head of the high seminary answered in firm tones :

"Let us, Monseigneur, if you please, drop the subject of the trade to which the friend of M. Worms-Clavelin, the Jewish *préfet*, devotes himself, and allow me to enumerate the only too definite complaints which I have to bring against the professor of rhetoric at the high seminary.   I impugn : first, his doctrine ; second, his conduct.   I say that I indict first his doctrine, and that on four grounds : first . . ."

The Cardinal-Archbishop stretched out both his arms as though to ward off such a multitude of charges.

"Monsieur Lantaigne, I see that for some time the vicar-general has been biting his pen and making desperate signs to remind me that our printer is waiting for our pastoral letter, which has to be read on Sunday in the churches of our diocese. Allow me to finish dictating this charge, which, I trust, will bring some solace to our priests and faithful people."

Abbé Lantaigne bowed, and very sadly withdrew. After his departure the Cardinal-Archbishop, turning to M. de Goulet, said :

" I did not know that M. Guitrel was so friendly with the *préfet*. And I am grateful to the head of the seminary for having warned me of it. M. Lantaigne is sincerity itself : I prize his frankness and straightforwardness. With him, one knows where one is . . ."

He corrected himself :

"Where one would be."

II

LANTAIGNE, principal of the high seminary, was working in his study, the whitewashed walls of which were three parts covered by deal shelves loaded with the dark bindings of his working library, the whole of Migne's *Patrologie,* and cheap editions of Saint Thomas Aquinas, Baronius and Bossuet. A Virgin in the manner of Mignard surmounted the door, with a dusty sprig of box sticking out of the old gilt frame. Uninviting horsehair chairs stood on the red tiles in front of the windows, through which the stale smell of the refectory ascended to the cotton window-curtains.

The principal, bending over his little walnut-wood desk, was turning over the pages of the registers handed him by Abbé Perruque, the master of method, who stood at his side.

" I see," said M. Lantaigne, " that again this week a hoard of sweetmeats has been discovered in a pupil's room. Such infractions are far too often repeated."

In fact, the students of the seminary made a practice of hiding cakes of chocolate among their school-books. This was what they called theology *Menier*. They used to meet in a room at night, by twos or threes, to discuss it.

M. Lantaigne begged the master of method to use unfaltering severity.

"This disorder is deplorable in that it may involve the most serious misconduct."

He asked for the register of the rhetoric class. But when M. Perruque had handed it to him, he looked away from it. His heart swelled at the idea that sacred rhetoric was taught by this Guitrel, a man with neither morals nor learning. He sighed within himself:

"When will the scales fall from the Cardinal-Archbishop's eyes, that he may see the unworthiness of this priest?"

Then, tearing himself from this bitter thought only to plunge into the bitterness of another:

"And Piédagnel?" he asked.

For two years Firmin Piédagnel had caused incessant anxiety to the head of the seminary. The only son of a cobbler who kept his stall between two buttresses of Saint-Exupère, he was, through the brightness of his intelligence, the most brilliant pupil in the house. Of placid temperament, he had a very fair report for conduct. The timidity of his character

B

and the weakness of his constitution seemed a good safeguard for his moral purity. But he had neither the instinct for theology nor the vocation for the priesthood. His very faith was unstable. With his great spiritual knowledge, M. Lantaigne had no inordinate fear of those violent crises among his young Levites, which, often salutary, are to be allayed by grace. He dreaded, on the contrary, the indifference of a placidly intractable mind. He almost despaired of a soul to whom doubt was light and bearable and whose thoughts flowed to irreligion by a natural inclination. Such a one the shoemaker's clever son showed himself to be. M. Lantaigne had one day unexpectedly chanced, by one of those brusque wiles which were natural to him, to plumb the depths of this nature, double-faced through its courtesy. He perceived with consternation that from the teaching at the seminary Firmin had only acquired an elegant Latin style, skill in sophistry, and a kind of sentimental mysticism. From that time Firmin had appeared to him as a being weak and formidable, pitiable and noxious. Yet he loved this lad, loved him tenderly, to infatuation. In spite of his disappointment it pleased him that he should be the honour, the glory of the seminary. He loved in Firmin the charm of his mind, the subtle harmony of his style, and even the tenderness of those pale, short-sighted eyes, like bruises

under the quivering eyelids.   He sometimes took
pleasure in seeing in him one of the victims of this
Abbé Guitrel, whose intellectual and moral poverty
must (so he firmly believed) injure and depress an intelligent and quick-sighted pupil.   He flattered himself
that, if better trained in the future, Firmin, although
too weak ever to give to the Church one of those
powerful leaders whom she so much needs, would at
least produce for religion, perhaps, a Péreyve or a
Gerbet, one of those priests who carry into the priesthood the heart of a young mother.   But, incapable
of long self-flattery, M. Lantaigne speedily rejected
this unlikely hope and saw in this lad a Guéroult, a
Renan.   And the sweat of anguish chilled his forehead.   His fear was lest, in rearing such pupils,
he might be training formidable enemies of the
truth.

He knew that it was in the temple itself that
the hammers were forged which overthrew it.
He very often said : " Such is the power of theological discipline that it alone is capable of rearing
great reprobates ; an unbeliever who has not passed
through our hands is powerless and without weapons
for evil.   It is within our walls that they imbibe all
knowledge, even that of blasphemy."   From the
mass of the students he only demanded industry and
integrity, feeling certain that these would make good
parish priests of them.   But in his finest students

he feared curiosity, pride, the impious boldness of the intellect, and even the qualities that brought the angels to perdition.

"Monsieur Perruque," said he brusquely, "let us see the notes on Piédagnel."

The master of method, with his thumb moistened at his lips, turned over the leaves of the register, and then pointed out with his great dirt-encircled forefinger the lines traced on the margin of the book :

M. Piédagnel holds thoughtless conversations.

M. Piédagnel gives way to depression.

M. Piédagnel refuses to take any physical exercise.

The director read and shook his head. He turned the leaf and continued reading :

M. Piédagnel has written a poor essay on the unity of the faith.

At this Abbé Lantaigne burst out :

"Unity—that is just what he will never grasp ! And yet it is the idea above all others which ought to be impressed on the priest's mind. For I do not fear to affirm that this conception is entirely of God, and, as it were, His most vivid manifestation among men."

He turned his hollow, gloomy gaze towards Abbé Perruque.

"This subject of the unity of the faith, Monsieur Perruque, is my touchstone by which I try the spirits.   The simplest minds, if they do not fail in sincerity, draw logical conclusions from the idea of unity ; and the most able derive an admirable philosophy from this principle.   In the pulpit, Monsieur Perruque, I have three times handled the unity of the faith, and the wealth of the subject still amazes me."

He resumed his reading :

M. Piédagnel has compiled a note-book, which has been found in his desk, and which contains, written in M. Piédagnel's own hand, extracts from different love-poems, composed by Leconte de Lisle and Paul Verlaine, as well as by several other loose writers, and the choice of the extracts betrays excessive profligacy both of the mind and the senses.

He shut the register and pushed it away roughly. "What we lack nowadays," sighed he, "is neither learning nor intelligence; it is the theological mind."

"Monsieur," said Abbé Perruque, "the steward wants to know if you can receive him at once.   The contract with Lafolie for butcher's meat expires on the fifteenth of this month, and they are waiting for your decision before renewing an arrangement upon which the house can scarcely plume itself.   For you cannot fail to have remarked the bad quality of the beef supplied by Lafolie."

"Tell the steward to come in," said M. Lantaigne.

And, left alone, he put his head in his hands and sighed :

"*O quando finieris et quando cessabis, universa vanitas mundi ?* * Far from Thee, O God, we are but wandering shadows. There are no greater crimes than those committed against the unity of the faith. Vouchsafe to lead the world back to this blessed unity !"

When, during the recreation hour after the mid-day meal, the principal crossed the courtyard, the seminarists were playing a game of football. On the gravelled playground there was a great commotion of ruddy heads poised on stalks like black knife-handles, the jerky gestures of puppets, and shouts and cries in all the rustic dialects of the diocese. The master of method, Abbé Perruque, his cassock tucked up, was joining in the game with the zest of a cloistered peasant, drunk with air and exercise, and in athletic style was kicking from the toe of his buckled shoe the huge ball covered with its leather quarters. At sight of the principal the players stopped. M. Lantaigne made a sign to them to continue. He followed the grove of stunted acacia trees that fringes the courtyard on the side towards the ramparts and the country. Half-way along he met three pupils who, arm in arm,

* " When wilt thou end, when wilt thou cease to be, oh, ever-present vanity of this world ? "

were walking up and down as they talked. Since they usually spent the recreation hours in this way, they were called the peripatetics. M. Lantaigne called one of them, the shortest, a pale-faced lad, with slightly stooping shoulders, a refined and mocking mouth, and timid eyes. He did not hear at first, and his neighbour had to nudge him with an elbow and say to him :

"Piédagnel, the principal is calling you."

At this Piédagnel approached Abbé Lantaigne and bowed to him with a half-graceful clumsiness.

"My child," said the principal to him, "you will be so good as to be my server at mass to-morrow."

The young man blushed. It was a coveted honour to serve the principal's mass.

Abbé Lantaigne, his breviary under his arm, went out by the little door that opens on the fields and took the customary road in his walks, a dusty track edged with nettles and thistles that follows the ramparts.

He was thinking :

"What will become of this poor child, if he is suddenly expelled, ignorant of any sort of manual labour, weak, delicate, and timid ? And what grief there will be in his infirm father's shop ! "

He walked along over the flints of the barren road. Having reached the mission cross, he took off his hat, wiped the perspiration from his fore-

head with his silk handkerchief, and said in a
low voice :

"Oh God, inspire me to act according to Thy
interests, whatever it may cost my paternal heart !"

At half-past six next morning Abbé Lantaigne was
saying the concluding words of the mass in the bare,
deserted chapel.

In front of a side-altar a solitary old sacristan was
setting paper flowers in porcelain vases, beneath the
gilt statue of Saint Joseph.   A grey, rainy daylight
poured sadly through the blurred window-panes.   The
celebrant, upright at the left of the high altar, was
reading the last Gospel.

" *Et Verbum caro factum est,*" said he, bending his
knees.

Firmin Piédagnel, who was serving the mass, knelt
at the same time on the step where stood the bell ;
then he rose and, after the last responses, preceded
the priest into the sacristy.   Abbé Lantaigne set down
the chalice with the corporal and waited for the
server to help him remove his priestly vestments.
Firmin Piédagnel, being sensitive to the mysterious
influences of things, felt the charm of this scene, so
simple and yet so sacred.   His soul, suffused with
tender unction, tasted with a kind of joy the familiar
grandeur of the priesthood.   Never had he felt so
deeply the desire to be a priest and in his turn to
celebrate the holy sacrifice.   Having kissed and

carefully folded up the alb and chasuble, he bowed before Abbé Lantaigne ere retiring.   The head of the seminary, who had resumed his great-coat, made a sign to him to stay, and looked at him with such nobility and kindness that the young man received the look as a favour and a blessing.   After a long silence :

"My child," said M. Lantaigne, "whilst cele-brating this mass which I asked you to serve, I prayed God to give me the strength to send you away.   My prayer has been granted.   You are no longer a member of this household."

As he took in these words, Firmin was stupefied. It seemed to him that the flooring was giving way beneath his feet.   Through eyes big with tears, he vaguely saw the lonely road, the rain, a life darkened with misery and toil, the fate of a lost child terrified by its own weakness and timidity.   He looked at M. Lantaigne.   The resolute gentleness, the quiet strength, the calmness of this man revolted him. Suddenly a feeling was born and grew in him, a feeling that sustained and strengthened him, a hatred of the priest, a deathless and fruitful hatred, a hatred to fill a whole life.   Without uttering a word, he went with great strides out of the sacristy.

III

BBE LANTAIGNE, head of the nigh
seminary of . . ., wrote the follow-
ing letter to Monseigneur the Cardinal-Archbishop of . . . :

" Monseigneur,

" When, on the 17th of this month, I had the
honour of being received by Your Eminence, I
feared to trespass on your paternal kindness and
on your pastoral clemency by expounding at sufficient
length the matter about which I came to converse
with you. But as this affair reflects on your high
and holy jurisdiction and concerns the government
of this diocese, which counts among the most ancient
and beautiful provinces of Christian Gaul, I conceive
it to be my duty to submit to the watchful im-
partiality of Your Eminence the facts concerning
which it is called upon to judge in the plenitude of
its authority and in the fulness of its wisdom.

" In bringing these facts to the knowledge of
Your Eminence, I am fulfilling a duty which I should
characterise as painful to my heart, if I did not

know that the accomplishment of every duty brings to the soul an inexhaustible spring of consolation, and that it is not enough to obey God, if one does not obey Him with ready gladness.

"The facts which it behoves you to know, Monseigneur, relate to Abbé Guitrel, professor of rhetoric at the high seminary. I will state them as briefly and as accurately as possible.

" These facts concern :

" First, the doctrine ;

" Second, the morals of Abbé Guitrel.

" I will first state the facts relating to M. Guitrel's doctrine.

" On reading the note-books from which he delivers his lectures on sacred rhetoric, I noticed in them various opinions which do not agree with the tradition of the Church.

" First, M. Guitrel, whilst condemning as to their conclusions the commentaries on Holy Scripture drawn up by atheists and so-called reformers, does not condemn them in their principle and origin, in which he is seriously in error. For it is evident that, the care of the Scriptures having been confided to the Church, the Church alone is capable of inter- preting the books which she alone preserves.

" Second, led astray by the recent example of a monk who thirsted for the applause of the age, M. Guitrel presumes to explain the scenes of the

Gospel by means of that pretended local colour and that pseudo-psychology of which the Germans make a great show ; and he does not perceive that, by thus walking in the way of infidels, he is skirting the abyss into which they have fallen. I should weary the benevolent attention of His Eminence Monseigneur the Cardinal-Archbishop were I to place before his reverend glance the passages where M. Guitrel with pitiable childishness follows the narratives of travellers, as to 'the boat-service on the Lake of Tiberias,' and those where, with intolerable indecency, he describes what he calls 'the soul-states' and 'the psychic crises' of our Lord Jesus Christ.

"These foolish innovations, blameworthy in a cloistered worldling, should not be tolerated in a secular cleric entrusted with the instruction of young aspirants to the priesthood. Hence I was more grieved than surprised when I heard that an intelligent pupil, whom I have since been obliged to expel for his bad disposition, described the professor of rhetoric as a 'fin de siècle' priest.

"Third, M. Guitrel affects a culpable laxity in relying on the untrustworthy authority of Clement of Alexandria, who is not included in the martyrology. In this the professor of rhetoric betrays the weakness of a mind misled by the example of the so-called mystics, who imagine that they find in the

Stromata a purely allegorical interpretation of the most concrete mysteries of the Christian faith. And, without actually going astray, M. Guitrel shows himself, in this matter, to be inconsistent and light-minded.

" Fourth, since depravity of taste is one of the results of doctrinal weakness, and since a mind which rejects strong food battens on worthless nourishment, M. Guitrel seeks models of eloquence for the use of his pupils even in the speeches of M. Lacordaire and the homilies of M. Gratry.

" Secondly, I will enumerate the facts relating to M. Guitrel's morals.

" First, Abbé Guitrel consorts with M. *le préfet* Worms-Clavelin both secretly and constantly, and in this he throws off the reserve which it always behoves an ecclesiastic of lower rank to observe in relation to the public authorities, a reserve which, under present circumstances and towards a Jewish official, there is no excuse for dropping. And by the care which he takes never to enter the prefecture save by a private door, M. Guitrel seems to acknowledge to himself the falseness of a position which he nevertheless maintains.

" It is also notorious that M. Guitrel occupies a position with respect to Madame Worms-Clavelin that is more mercantile than religious. This lady is fond of antiquities, and although a Jewess, she does not despise any articles connected with religion, provided that they have the merit of art or of antiquity. It is unhappily well attested that M. Guitrel busies himself in buying for Madame Worms-Clavelin at an absurd price the antique furniture of village parsonages, left in the care of ignorant churchwardens. In this way carved wainscoting, priestly vestments, chalices, and pyxes are torn from the sacristies of your rural churches, Monseigneur, in order that at the prefecture they may adorn the private apartments of M. and Madame Worms-Clavelin. And everybody knows that Madame Worms-Clavelin has trimmed with the splendid and sacred copes of Saint-Porchaire the species of furniture vulgarly called '*poufs*.' I do not imply that M. Guitrel has derived any material and direct profit from these transactions ; but it must needs grieve your paternal heart that a priest of the diocese should have joined in robbing your churches of that wealth which proves, even in the eyes of unbelievers, the superiority of Christian to profane art.

"Second, without complaint or protest Abbé Guitrel allows the rumour to spread and grow that his elevation to the vacant bishopric of Tourcoing is favoured by the President of the Council, the Minister for Justice and Religion. Now this rumour is prejudicial to the minister, for, although a freethinker and a freemason, he ought to be too careful of the interests of the Church over which he has been appointed civil overseer to place in the seat of the blessed Loup a priest such as M. Guitrel. And if this invention were to be traced to its source, it is to be feared that in M. Guitrel himself would be found the first and foremost contriver of it.

"Third, having formerly occupied his leisure in translating into French verse the Bucolics of that Latin poet called Calpurnius, whom the best critics agree in relegating to the lowest class of insipid babblers, Abbé Guitrel, with a carelessness which I would fain believe to be quite unintentional, has allowed this work of his youth to circulate privately. A copy of the Bucolics was addressed to the free-thinking radical paper of the district, *le Phare*, which published extracts from it ; among them there occurred in particular this line, which I blush to put before the paternal eyes of Your Eminence :

"And our heaven of bliss is a well-loved breast.*

"This quotation was accompanied in *le Phare* by the most derogatory comments on the private character, as well as the literary taste, of Abbé Guitrel. And the editor, whose ill-will is only too well known to Your Eminence, took this wretched line as a pretext for charges of wanton thoughts and dishonourable intentions generally against all the professors of the high

* "Notre ciel à nous, c'est un sein chéri."

seminary, and even against all the priests in the diocese. This is why, without inquiring whether as a scholar M. Guitrel had any excuse for translating Calpurnius, I deplore the publication of his work as the cause of a scandal which, I am sure, was more bitter to your benevolent heart, Monseigneur, than gall and wormwood.

"Fourth, M. Guitrel is in the habit of going every day at five o'clock in the afternoon to the confectioner's shop kept by Dame Magloire, in the Place Saint-Exupère. And there, leaning over the sideboards, counters and tables, he examines with deep interest and careful diligence the dainties piled up on plates and dishes. Then, stopping at the spot where are arranged the kinds of cakes which they tell me are called *éclairs* and *babas*, he touches first one and then another of these pasties with the tip of his finger, and afterwards has these dainty morsels wrapped up in a sheet of paper. Far be it from me to bring a charge of sensuality against him on account of this ridiculously careful choice of a few cream-cakes or sugar-pasties. But if one reflects that he goes to Dame Magloire's at the very moment when the shop is thronged with fashionable folk of both sexes, and that he makes himself a butt for the jests of worldlings, one will ask oneself whether the professor of rhetoric at the high seminary does not leave some part of his dignity behind him in the confectioner's shop. In fact, the choice of two cakes has not escaped the ill-natured comment of observers, and it is said, either rightly or wrongly, that M. Guitrel keeps one for himself and gives the other to his servant. He may doubtless, without incurring any blame, share any dainties with the woman attached to his service, especially if that woman has attained the canonical age. But malicious gossip interprets this intimacy and familiarity in the most shameful sense, and I should never dare to repeat to Your Eminence the remarks which are made in the town as to the relations between M. Guitrel and his domestic. I do not wish to entertain these charges. Nevertheless, Your Eminence will see that M. Guitrel is not easily to be excused for having given a show of truth to the calumny by his mischievous behaviour. I have related the facts. It now remains for me only to conclude.

"I have the honour to propose that Your Eminence should cancel the appointment of M. Guitrel (Joachim) as professor of sacred rhetoric at the high seminary of . . ., in accordance with your spiritual powers as recognised by the State (decree of 17th March, 1808).

"Vouchsafe, Monseigneur, to continue your paternal kindness towards one who, being placed in command of your seminary, has no dearer wish than to give you proofs of his complete devotion

and of the profound respect with which he has
the honour to be,

"Monseigneur,
"The most humble and obedient servant
of Your Eminence,
"LANTAIGNE."

Having written this letter, M. Lantaigne sealed it
with his seal.

IV

T is true that Abbé Guitrel, professor of sacred rhetoric at the high seminary of . . ., was intimately connected with M. *le préfet* Worms-Clavelin and with Madame Worms-Clavelin, *née* Coblentz. But Abbé Lantaigne was wrong in believing that M. Guitrel frequented the drawing-rooms of the prefecture, where his presence would have been equally disquieting to the Archbishop and to the masonic lodges, since the *préfet* was master of the lodge "The Rising Sun." It was in the confectioner's shop kept by Dame Magloire in the Place Saint-Exupère, where he went every Saturday at five o'clock to buy two little three-sou cakes, one for his servant and the other for himself, that the priest had met the *préfet's* wife, while she was eating *babas* there in the company of Madame Lacarelle, wife of M. *le préfet's* private secretary.

By his demeanour, at once obsequious and discreet, which inspired entire confidence and removed all apprehensions, the professor of sacred rhetoric had instantly gained the good graces of Madame Worms-Clavelin, to whom he suggested the mind, the face, and almost the sex of those old-clothes women, the guardian angels of her youth in the difficult days of Batignolles and the Place Clichy, when Noémi Coblentz had finished growing up and was beginning to fade in the business office kept by her father Isaac in the midst of distress-sales and police-raids. One of these dealers in second-hand clothes, a Madame Vacherie, who esteemed her, had acted as go-between for her and an active and promising young barrister, M. Théodore Worms-Clavelin, who, finding her seriously-minded and practically useful, had married her after the birth of their daughter Jeanne, and she in return had cleverly pushed him in the administration. Abbé Guitrel was very much like Madame Vacherie. They had the same look, the same voice, the same gestures. This propitious likeness had aroused in Madame Worms-Clavelin a sudden sympathy. Besides, she had always revered the Catholic clergy as one of the powers of this world. She constituted herself M. Guitrel's advocate in her husband's good graces. M. Worms-Clavelin, who recognised in his wife a quality that remained him a deep mystery, the quality of tact, and who knew her to be clever, received Abbé Guitrel courteously the first time he met him in the jeweller's

shop kept by Rondonneau junior in the Rue des
Tintelleries.

He had gone there to see the designs for the
cups ordered by the State to be given as prizes in
the races organised by the Society for the Improve-
ment of Horse-breeding.   After that visit he frequently returned to the goldsmith's, drawn by an
innate taste for precious metals.   On his side, Abbé
Guitrel contrived frequent occasions for visiting the
show-rooms of Rondonneau the younger, maker of
sacred vessels : candlesticks, lamps, pyxes, chalices,
patens, monstrances, and tabernacles.   The *préfet* and
the priest were not ill-pleased at these meetings in
the first-storey show-rooms, out of sight of prying
eyes, in front of a counter loaded with bullion and
amidst the vases and statuettes that M. Worms-
Clavelin called *bondieuseries*.*   Stretched out in
Rondonneau junior's one arm-chair, M. Worms-
Clavelin sent a little wave of his hand to M. Guitrel,
who, black and fat, stole along by the glass cases like
a great rat.

"Good-day, monsieur l'abbé.   Delighted to see
you ! "

And it was true.   He vaguely felt that, in contact
with this ecclesiastic of peasant stock, as French in
priestly character and in type as the blackened stones
of Saint-Exupère and the old trees on the Mall,

* Lit. good-goderies—*i.e.*, pious gimcrackeries.

he was frenchifying himself, naturalising himself,
stripping off the ponderous remnants of his German
and Semitic descent. Intimacy with a priest was
flattering to the Jewish official. In it he tasted,
without actually acknowledging it to himself, the
pride of revenge. To browbeat, to patronise one
of those tonsured heads entrusted for eighteen
centuries, both by heaven and earth, with the ex-
communication and extermination of the circumcised,
was for the Jew a keen and flattering success. And
besides, this dirty, threadbare, yet respected, cassock
that bowed before him entered châteaux where the
préfet was not received. The aristocratic women of
the department revered this garb now humiliated
before the official uniform. Deference from one of
the clergy was almost equivalent to deference from
that rural nobility that had not completely come
over, and of whose scornful coldness the Jew,
though by no means sensitive, had had painful
experiences. M. Guitrel, humble, yet with *finesse*,
made his deference appreciated.

Being honoured as a powerful master by this
ecclesiastical politician, the head of the department
returned in patronage what he received in deference,
and flung conciliatory speeches at Abbé Guitrel:

"Doubtless there are good, devoted, and intelligent priests. When the clergy takes its stand upon
its privileges . . ."

And Abbé Guitrel bowed.

M. Worms-Clavelin went on:

"The Republic does not wage systematic war on the parish priests. And, if the fraternities had submitted to the law, many of their difficulties would have been avoided."

And M. Guitrel protested:

"It is a matter of principle. I should have decided in favour of the fraternities. It is also a matter of business. The fraternities did a great deal of good."

The *préfet* summed up from out of the cloud of his cigar-smoke.

"Harking back over what has been done is useless. But the new spirit is a spirit of conciliation."

And again M. Guitrel bowed, while Rondonneau junior bent over his account books his bald head where the flies pitched.

One day, being asked to give her opinion about a vase that the *préfet* was to present with his own hand to the winner in the race for draught-horses, Madame Worms-Clavelin came to Rondonneau junior's with her husband. She found M. Guitrel in the jeweller's office. He made a feint to leave the place. But they begged him to remain. They even consulted him as to the nymphs who formed, by their bending figures, the handles of the cup. The *préfet* would have preferred them to be Amazons.

"Amazons, doubtless," murmured the professor of sacred rhetoric.

Madame Worms-Clavelin would have liked centauresses.

"Centauresses, yes, yes," said the priest; "or rather centaurs."

Meanwhile Rondonneau junior was holding up the wax model in his fingers in front of the spectators and smiling in admiration.

"Monsieur l'abbé," asked the *préfet*, "does the Church always ban the nude in art ?"

M. Guitrel replied :

"The Church has never absolutely proscribed nude studies ; but she has always judiciously restrained their employment."

Madame Worms-Clavelin looked at the priest and thought how remarkably like Madame Vacherie he was. She confided to him that she had a passion for curios, that she was mad about brocades, stamped velvets, gold fringes, embroidery and lace. She disclosed to him the covetous desires accumulated in her mind since the days when she used to trail in her youth and poverty in front of the shop-windows of the second-hand dealers in the Quartier Bréda. She told him that she had dreams of a salon with old copes and old chasubles, and that she was also collecting antique jewels.

He answered that in truth the ornaments of the

priests provided precious models for artists, and that there we had a proof that the Church was no enemy to art.

From that day forward M. Guitrel began to hunt in the country sacristies for splendid antiques, and scarcely a week passed that he did not carry into Rondonneau junior's, under his great-coat, a chasuble or a cope, adroitly pillaged from some innocent priest. M. Guitrel was, moreover, very scrupulous in remitting to the rifled vestry-board the hundred-sou piece with which the *préfet* paid for the silk, the brocade, the velvet and the lace.

In six months' time Madame Worms-Clavelin's drawing-room had become like a cathedral treasury ; a clinging odour of incense lingered round it.

One summer day in that year, M. Guitrel, according to custom, mounted the goldsmith's stairs, and found M. Worms-Clavelin puffing away merrily in the shop. For the day before the *préfet* had succeeded in getting his candidate, a cattle-breeder, and young turn-coat royalist, returned; and he was counting on the approval of the minister, who secretly preferred the new to the old republicans as being less exacting and more humble. In the elation of his boisterous satisfaction, he slapped the priest on the shoulder :

" Monsieur l'abbé, what we want is many priests like you, enlightened, tolerant, free from prejudices—

for you haven't any prejudices, not you !—priests who recognise the needs of the present day and the requirements of a democratic society. If the episcopate, if the French clergy would only catch the progressive yet conservative sentiments that the Republic professes, they would still have a fine part to play."

Then, amidst the smoke of his big cigar, he expounded ideas on religion which testified to an ignorance that filled M. Guitrel with inward dismay. The *préfet*, however, declared himself to be more Christian than many Christians, and in the language of the masonic lodge he extolled the moral teaching of Jesus, while he rejected indiscriminately local superstitions and fundamental dogmas, the needles thrown into the piscina of Saint Phal by marriageable girls, and the real presence in the Eucharist.

M. Guitrel, an easy-going soul, but incapable of yielding a point as to dogma, stammered out :

"One must make a distinction, monsieur *le préfet*, one must make a distinction."

In order to make a diversion, he drew out from a pocket of his great-coat a roll of parchment which he opened on the counter. It was a large page of plainchant, with Gothic text under the four-line divisions, with rubrics and a decorated initial.

The *préfet* fixed his great, lamp-globe eyes on the page. Rondonneau junior, stretching out his rosy bald head, said :

"The miniature in the initial is rather fine.   It's Saint Agatha, isn't it ? "

"The martyrdom of Saint Agatha," said M. Guitrel. " Here are seen the executioners torturing the breasts of the saint."

And he added in a voice which flowed as sweetly as thick syrup :

" According to authentic records, such was in fact the torment inflicted on Saint Agatha of blessed memory by the proconsul.   A page from an anti-phonary, Monsieur *le préfet*—a trifle, a mere trifle, which perhaps will find a little niche in the collections of Madame Worms-Clavelin, so devoted to our Christian antiquities.   This page gives us a fragment of the proper of the saint.

And he deciphered the Latin text, marking the tonic accent energetically :

" *Dum torqueretur beata Agata in mamillâ graviter dixit ad judicem : 'Impie, crudelis et dire tyranne, non es confusus amputare in feminâ quod ipse in matre suxisti? Ego habeo mamillas integras intus in animâ quas Domino consecravi.'"* *

The *préfet*, who was a graduate, half understood,

---

* " While the blessed Agatha was being cruelly tortured in the breast, she said to the judge : 'Oh, wicked, cruel, and savage tyrant, art thou not ashamed to mutilate in a woman that with which your mother fed you ?   Within my soul I have breasts undesecrated which I have sanctified to God.'"

and in his desire to appear Gallic, remarked that it was piquant.

"Naïve," answered Abbé Guitrel gently, "naïve."

M. Worms-Clavelin granted that the language of the Middle Ages had, in fact, a certain naïveté.

"It has also sublimity," said M. Guitrel.

But the *préfet* was rather inclined to seek in Church Latin for the piquancy of broad humour, and it was with a sly little laugh of obstinacy that he crammed the parchment into his pocket, with many thanks to his dear Guitrel for this discovery.

Then, pushing the Abbé into the window-recess, he whispered in his ear :

"My dear Guitrel, when the chance comes, I will do something for you."

V

THERE was one party in the town which openly declared that Abbé Lantaigne, principal of the high seminary, was a priest worthy of a bishopric and fitted to fill the vacant see of Tourcoing honourably, until the time when Monseigneur Charlot's death should enable him, cross in hand and amethyst on finger, to assume the mitre in the town that had witnessed his labours and his merits. This was the scheme of the venerable M. Cassignol, ex-president in chief, and a State pensioner of twenty-five years' standing. With these plans were associated M. Lerond, deputy attorney-general at the time of the decrees,* now a barrister practising at . . ., and Abbé de Lalonde, formerly an Army chaplain, and now chaplain to the Dames du Salut. These, belonging to the most respected, but not to the most influential, class in the town, made up practically the whole of Abbé Lantaigne's party. The head of the high seminary

* The *coup d'état* of 1851.

had been invited to dine with M. Cassignol, the chief president, who said to him, in the presence of M. de Lalonde and M. Lerond :

" Monsieur l'abbé, put yourself forward as a candidate.   When it shall come to a choice between Abbé Lantaigne, who has so nobly served both religion and Christian France by pen and tongue, who has protected the oft-betrayed cause of the rights of the French Church within the Catholic Church with the force of his mental endowments and high character, and M. Guitrel, none will have the effrontery to hesitate.   And since it seems that this time the honour of supplying a bishop for the town of Tourcoing is to fall to our city, the faithful of the diocese are willing to lose you for a time for the good of the episcopate as well as of Christendom."

And the venerable M. Cassignol, who was now in his eighty-sixth year, added with a smile :

" We shall see you again, I have a firm conviction of that.   You will come back to us from Tourcoing, monsieur l'abbé."

Abbé Lantaigne had replied :

" Monsieur *le président*, with no intention of anticipating any honour, I yet shall shirk no duty."

He yearned and longed for the see of the lamented Monseigneur Duclou.   But this priest, whose ambition was frozen by his pride, was waiting until they came to bring him the mitre.

One morning M. Lerond came to see him at the seminary, and brought news of how Abbé Guitrel's candidature was progressing at the Ministry of Public Worship. It was suspected that M. *le préfet* Worms-Clavelin was working hard in favour of M. Guitrel in the offices of the Ministry, where all the freemasons had already received their orders. This was what he had been told at the offices of *le Libéral*, the religious and moderate paper of the district. With regard to the intentions of the Cardinal-Archbishop, nothing was known.

The truth was that Monseigneur Charlot dared neither oppose nor support any candidate. His characteristic caution had been growing on him for years. If he had any preferences he let no one guess them. For a long time he had been comfortably and pleasurably concealing his policy, just as he played his game of bezique every evening with M. de Goulet. And, in fact, the promotion of a priest of his diocese to a non-suffragan bishopric was in no way an affair of his. But he was forced to take part in this intrigue. M. Worms-Clavelin, the *préfet*, whom he did not wish to offend, had caused him to be sounded. His Eminence could not be ignorant of the shrewd and urbane disposition of which M. Guitrel had given plain proofs in the diocese. On the other hand, he believed this Guitrel to be capable of anything. "Who knows," thought he, "whether he is not

scheming to get himself appointed here as my coadjutor, instead of going to that gloomy little metropolis
of Northern Gaul ?   And if I declare him worthy of
a bishopric, will it not be believed that I intend him
to share my see ?" This apprehension that he would
be given a coadjutor embittered Monseigneur Charlot's
old age.   In Abbé Lantaigne's case he had strong
reasons for being silent and holding aloof.   He would
not have supported this priest's candidature for the
simple reason that he foresaw its failure.   Monseigneur Charlot never willingly put himself on the
losing side.   Moreover, he loathed the principal of
the high seminary.   Yet this hatred, in a mind so
easy-going and kindly as Monseigneur's, was not
actually prejudicial to M. Lantaigne's ambitions.
In order to get rid of him, Monseigneur Charlot
would have consented to his becoming either bishop
or Pope.   M. Lantaigne had a high reputation for
piety, learning, and eloquence : one could not,
without a certain shamelessness, be openly against
him.   Now Monseigneur Charlot, being popular
and very keen to gain every one's goodwill, did not
despise the opinion of honourable men.

M. Lerond was unable to follow the secret
thoughts of Monseigneur, but he knew that the
Archbishop had not yet committed himself.   He
judged that it might be possible to bring influence
to bear on the old man's mind and that an appeal

to his pastoral instincts might not be in vain.   He urged M. Lantaigne to proceed at once to the Archbishop's palace.

"You will beg His Eminence, with filial deference, for advice in the probable event of the bishopric of Tourcoing being offered to you.   It is the right step, and it will produce an excellent effect."

M. Lantaigne objected :

"It behoves me to wait for a more solemn call."

"What call could be more solemn than the suffrages of so many zealous Christians, who hail your name with a unanimity that recalls the ancient popular acclamations with which a Médard and a Remi were greeted ?"

"But, monsieur," answered honest Lantaigne, "those acclamations, in the obsolete custom to which you refer, came from the faithful of the diocese which these holy men were called upon to govern.   And I am not aware that the Catholics of Tourcoing have acclaimed me."

At this point lawyer Lerond said what had to be said :

"If you do not bar the road for him, M. Guitrel will become a bishop."

The next day M. Lantaigne had fastened over his shoulders his visiting cloak, the turned-back wing of which flapped on his sturdy back, the while on the road to the Archbishop's palace he besought his God

D

to spare the Church of France an unmerited disgrace.

His Eminence, at the moment when M. Lantaigne bowed before him, had just received a letter from the nunciature asking him for a confidential note about M. Guitrel. The nuncio made no secret of his liking for a priest reputed to be intelligent and zealous and capable of being useful in negotiations with the temporal power. His Eminence had immediately dictated to M. de Goulet a note in favour of the nuncio's protégé.

He exclaimed in his pleasant tremulous voice :

" Monsieur Lantaigne, how glad I am to see you ! "

" Monseigneur, I have come to ask Your Eminence for your paternal counsel in case the Holy Father, regarding me with favour, should nominate me . . ."

" Very happy to see you, Monsieur Lantaigne. You come just in the nick of time ! "

" I would venture, if Your Eminence did not deem me unworthy of . . ."

" You are, Monsieur Lantaigne, an eminent theologian and a priest of the highest possible learning in the canon law. You are an authority on knotty points of discipline. Your advice is precious on questions of the liturgy and, in general, on any point that concerns religion. If you had not come, I was going to send for you, as M. de Goulet can tell you. At the present moment I am in great need of your insight."

And Monseigneur, with his gouty hand, well practised in benediction, waved the principal of the high seminary to a seat.

" Monsieur Lantaigne, be kind enough to listen to me. The venerable M. Laprune, the curé of Saint-Exupère, is just gone from here. I must tell you that this poor curé has this morning found a man hanged in his church. Just conceive his distress ! He is beside himself. And in such a crisis, I myself need to take the advice of the most learned priest in my diocese. What ought we to do ? Tell me ! "

M. Lantaigne collected himself for a moment. Then, in the tone of a pedagogue, he began to expound the traditions concerning the purification of churches :

" The Maccabees, after having washed the temple profaned by Antiochus Epiphanes, in the year 164 before the Incarnation, celebrated its dedication. That is the origin, Monseigneur, of the festival called Hanicha—that is to say, renewal. In fact . . ."

And he developed his ideas.

Monseigneur listened with an air of admiration, and M. Lantaigne drew up from his inexhaustible memory endless texts relating to the ceremonies of purification, precedents, arguments, commentaries.

"John, Chapter X., verse 22 . . . the Roman Pontifical . . . the Venerable Bede, Baronius . . ."

He spoke for three-quarters of an hour.

After this the Cardinal-Archbishop replied :

"It should be noted that the hanged man was found in the porch of the side door, on the epistle side."

"Was the inner door of the porch closed ? " asked M. Lantaigne.

"Alas ! alas ! " answered Monseigneur, " it was not wide open . . . but neither was it completely shut."

"Ajar, Monseigneur ? "

"That's it !   Ajar."

"And the suicide, Monseigneur, was within the space covered by the porch ?   That is a point which it is materially important to ascertain.   Your Eminence perceives the whole importance of that ? "

"Assuredly, Monsieur Lantaigne. . . .   Monsieur de Goulet, was there not one arm of the hanged man which projected from the porch and jutted into the church ? "

M. de Goulet replied with a blush and some incoherent syllables.

" I feel certain," replied Monseigneur, "that the arm went beyond, or, at any rate, part of the arm."

M. Lantaigne concluded from this that the church of Saint-Exupère was profaned.   He quoted precedents and described the proceedings after the dastardly assassination of the Archbishop of Paris, in the church of Saint-Étienne-du-Mont. He travelled up the ages, passed through the Revolution, when the churches were transformed into armouries, referred to Thomas Becket and the impious Heliodorus.

"What scholarship!   What sound doctrine!" said Monseigneur.

He rose and stretched out his hand for the priest to kiss.

"It is a priceless service that you have rendered me, Monsieur Lantaigne ; be assured that I have a great esteem for your scholarship and accept my pastoral benediction.   Farewell."

And M. Lantaigne, dismissed, perceived that he had not been able to say a single word about the important business on which he had come. But, with the echoes of his own words all round him, full of his learning and his application of it, and much flattered, he descended the grand staircase still turning over in his own mind the matter of the suicide of Saint-Exupère and the urgent need for the purification of the parish church.   Outside he was still thinking of it.

As he was descending the winding street of the Tintelleries, he met the curé of Saint-Exupère, the venerable M. Laprune, who, standing in front of cooper Lenfant's shop, was examining the corks.

His wine had been turning sour, and this deterioration he attributed to the defective way in which his bottles were corked.

"It is deplorable," he murmured, "deplorable!"

"And your suicide?" demanded Abbé Lantaigne.

At this question the worthy curé of Saint-Exupère opened his full, round eyes and asked in astonishment:

"What suicide?"

"The man who hanged himself in Saint-Exupère, the miserable suicide whom you found this morning in the porch of your church."

M. Laprune, terrified, wondering from what he had just heard, whether he or M. Lantaigne had gone mad, replied that he had found no one hanged.

"What!" replied M. Lantaigne, surprised in his turn, "wasn't a man found this morning hanged in the porch of a door on the epistle side!"

In sign of denial, the vicar twice revolved on his shoulders a face whereon shone the sacred truth.

Abbé Lantaigne now looked like a man taken with giddiness:

"But it was the Cardinal-Archbishop who has just told me himself that you found a man hanged in your church!"

"Oh!" replied M. Laprune, suddenly reassured, "Monseigneur wanted to amuse himself. He loves a jest. He is a capital hand at it, and knows how to keep within the bounds of seemliness. He has so much wit ! "

But Abbé Lantaigne, raising heavenwards his fiery, sombre glance, exclaimed :

"The Archbishop has deceived me ! This man will, then, never speak the truth, save when on the steps of the altar, taking the consecrated host in his hands, he pronounces the words : *Domine, non sum dignus !* "

VI

OW that he was no longer inclined to the saddle and liked to keep his room, General Cartier de Chalmot had reduced his division to cards in small cardboard boxes, which he placed every morning on his desk, and which he arranged every evening on the white deal shelves above his iron bedstead. He marshalled his cards day by day with scrupulous exactitude, in an order which filled him with satisfaction. Every card represented a man. The symbol by which he henceforth thought of his officers, non-commissioned officers and men, satisfied his craving for method and suited his natural bent of mind. Cartier de Chalmot had always been noted as an excellent officer. General Parroy, under whom he had served, said of him : " In Captain de Chalmot the capacity for obedience is exactly balanced by the power of command. A rare and priceless quality of the true military spirit."

Cartier de Chalmot had always been scrupulous

in the performance of his duty. Being upright, diffident, and an excellent penman, he had at last hit upon a system which fitted in with his abilities, and, in command of his division of cards, he applied his method with the utmost vigour.

On this particular day, having risen according to his custom at five o'clock in the morning, he had passed from his tub to his work-table ; and, whilst the sun was mounting with solemn slowness above the elms of the Archbishop's palace, the general was organising manœuvres by manipulating the boxes of cards that symbolised reality, and that were actually identical with reality to an intelligence which, like his, was excessively reverent towards everything symbolic.

For more than three hours he had been poring over his cards with a mind and face as wan and melancholy as the cards themselves, when his servant announced the Abbé de Lalonde. Then he took off his glasses, wiped his work-reddened eyes, rose, and half smiling, turned towards the door a countenance which had once been handsome and which in old age remained quite simple in its lineaments. He stretched out to the visitor who entered a large hand the palm of which had scarcely any lines, and said good-day to the priest in a gruff, yet hesitating voice, which revealed at the same time the diffidence of the man and the infallibility of the commander.

"My dear abbé, how are you? I am very glad to see you."

And he pushed forward to him one of the two horsehair chairs which, with the desk and the bed, comprised all the furniture of this clean, bright, empty room.

The abbé sat down. He was a wonderfully active little old man. In his face of weather-worn, crumbling brick, there were set, like two jewels, the blue eyes of a child.

They looked at one another for a moment, understandingly, without saying a word. They were two old friends, two comrades-in-arms. Formerly a chaplain in the Army, Abbé de Lalonde was now chaplain to the Dames du Salut. As military chaplain, he had been attached to the regiment of guards of which Cartier de Chalmot had been colonel in 1870, and which, forming part of the division . . ., had been shut up in Metz with Bazaine's army.

The memory of these homeric, yet lamentable, weeks came back to the minds of these two friends every time they saw one another, and every time they made the same remarks.

This time the chaplain began :

"Do you remember, general, when we were in Metz, running short of medicine, of fodder, running short of salt? . . ."

Abbé de Lalonde was the least sensual of men. He had hardly felt the want of salt for himself, but he had suffered much at not being able to give the men salt as he gave them tobacco, in little packets carefully wrapped up. And he remembered this cruel privation.

"Ah! general, the salt ran short!"

General Cartier de Chalmot replied :

"They made up for it, to a certain extent, by mixing gunpowder with the food."

"All the same," answered the chaplain, "war is a terrible thing."

Thus spoke this innocent friend of soldiers in the sincerity of his heart. But the general did not acquiesce in this condemnation of war.

"Pardon me, my dear abbé! War is, of course, a cruel necessity, but one which provides for officers and men an opportunity of showing the highest qualities. Without war, we should still be ignorant of how far the courage and endurance of men can go."

And, very seriously, he added :

"The Bible proves the lawfulness of war, and you know better than I how in it God is called Sabaoth— that is, the God of armies."

The abbé smiled with an expression of frank roguishness, displaying the three very white teeth which were all that remained to him.

"Pooh ! I don't know Hebrew, not I. . . . And God has so many more beautiful names that I can dispense with calling him by that one. . . . Alas ! general, what a splendid army perished under the command of that unhappy marshal ! . . ."

At these words, General Cartier de Chalmot began to say what he had already said a hundred times :

"Bazaine ! . . . Listen to me. Neglect of the regulations touching fortified towns, culpable hesitation in giving orders, mental reservations before the enemy. And before the enemy one ought to have no mental reservations. . . . Capitulation in open country. . . . He deserved his fate. And then a scapegoat was needed."

" For my part," answered the chaplain, " I should beware of ever saying a single word which might injure the memory of this unfortunate marshal. I cannot judge his actions. And it is certainly not my business to noise abroad even his indubitable shortcomings. For he granted me a favour for which I shall feel grateful as long as I live."

" A favour ? " demanded the general. " He ? To you ? "

"Oh ! a favour so noble, so beautiful ! He granted me a pardon for a poor soldier, a dragoon condemned to death for insubordination. In memory of this favour, every year I say a mass for the repose of the soul of ex-Marshal Bazaine."

But General Cartier de Chalmot would not let himself be turned from the point.

"Capitulation in open country ! . . . Just imagine it. . . . He deserved his fate."

And, in order to hearten himself up, the general spoke of Canrobert, and of the splendid stand of the . . . brigade at Saint-Privat.

And the chaplain related anecdotes of a diverting kind, with an edifying climax.

"Ah ! Saint-Privat, general ! On the eve of the battle, a great rascal of a carabineer came to look for me. I see him still, all blackened, in a sheepskin. He cries to me : 'To-morrow's going to be warm work. I may leave my bones to rot there. Confess me, monsieur le curé, and quickly ! I must go and groom my little mare.' I say to him : 'I don't want to delay you, friend. Still, you must tell me your sins. What are your sins ?' In astonishment he looks at me and replies : 'Why, all ! ' 'What, all ?' 'Yes, all. I have committed all the sins.' I shake my head. 'All, my friend—that is a good many ! . . . Tell me, hast thou beaten thy mother ?' At this question, my gentleman grows excited, waves his great arms, swears like a Pagan, and exclaims : 'Monsieur le curé, you are mocking me !' I reply to him : 'Calm yourself, friend. You see now that you have not committed all the sins.' . . ."

Thus the chaplain cheerily narrated pious regimental

anecdotes. And then he deduced the moral from them. Good Christians made good soldiers. It was a mistake to banish religion from the Army.

General Cartier de Chalmot approved of these maxims.

"I have always said so, my dear abbé. In destroying mystical beliefs you ruin the military spirit. By what right do you exact of a man the sacrifice of his life if you take away from him the hope of another existence ?"

And the chaplain answered, with a smile full of kindliness, innocence and joy :

"You will see that there will be a return to religion. They are already going back to it on all sides. Men are not as bad as they appear and God is infinitely good."

Then at last he revealed the object of his visit.

"I come, general, to ask a great favour of you."

General Cartier de Chalmot became attentive ; his face, already sad, grew sadder still. He loved and respected this old chaplain, and would have wished to give him pleasure. But the very idea of granting a favour was alarming to his strict upright= ness.

"Yes, general, I come to ask you to work for the good of the Church. You know Abbé Lantaigne, head of the high seminary in our town. He is a priest renowned for his piety and learning, a great theologian."

" I have met Abbé Lantaigne several times.   He made a favourable impression on me.   But . . ."

" Oh ! general, if you had heard his lectures as I have done, you would be amazed at his learning. Yet I was able to appreciate but a trifling part of it. Thirty years of my life I have spent in reminding poor soldiers stretched on a hospital bed of the goodness of God.   I have slipped in a good word along with a screw of tobacco.   For another twenty-five years I have been confessing holy maidens, full of sanctity, of course, but less charming in character than were my soldiers.   I have never had the time to read the Fathers ; I have neither enough brain nor enough theology to appreciate M. l'abbé Lantaigne at his true worth, for he is a walking encyclopedia. But at least I can assure you, general, that he speaks as he acts, and he acts as he speaks."

And the old chaplain, winking his eye roguishly, added :

" All ecclesiastics, unfortunately, are not of this kind."

" Nor are all soldiers," said the general, smiling a very wan smile.

And the two men exchanged a sympathetic glance, in their common hatred of intrigue and falsity.

Abbé de Lalonde, who was, however, capable of a

little guile, wound up his eulogy of Abbé Lantaigne with this touch :

"He is an excellent priest, and if he had been a soldier he would have made an excellent soldier."

But the general demanded brusquely :

"Well ! what can I do for him ?"

"Help him to slip on the violet stockings, which he has richly deserved, general.   He is an admitted candidate for the vacant bishopric of Tourcoing.   I beg you to support him with the Minister of Justice and Religion, whom, I am told, you know personally."

The general shook his head.   In fact, he had never asked anything of the Government.   Cartier de Chalmot, as a royalist and a Christian, regarded the Republic with a disapproval that was complete, silent and whole-hearted.   Reading no newspapers and talking with no one, he undervalued on principle a civil power of whose doings he knew nothing.   He obeyed and held his tongue.   He was admired in the châteaux of the neighbourhood for his melancholy resignation, inspired by the sentiment of duty, strengthened by a profound scorn for everything which was not military, intensified by a growing difficulty in thought and speech rendered obvious and affecting by the progress of an affection of the liver.

It was well known that General Cartier de Chalmot

remained a faithful royalist in the depths of his heart. It was not so well known that one day in the year 1893 his heart had received one of those shocks which can only be compared with what Christians describe as the workings of grace, and which bring with the force of a thunderbolt deep and unlooked-for peace to a man's innermost being. This event took place at five o'clock in the evening of the 4th of June in the drawing-rooms of the prefecture. There, among the flowers that Madame Worms-Clavelin had herself arranged, President Carnot, on his way through the town, had received the officers of the garrison. General Cartier de Chalmot, being present with his staff, saw the President for the first time, and instantly, for no apparent reason, on no explicable grounds, was pierced through and through by a terrible admiration. In a second, before the gentle gravity and honest inflexibility of the head of the State, all his prejudices fell away. He forgot that this sovereign was a civilian. He revered and loved him. He suddenly felt himself bound with ties of sympathy and respect to this man, sad and sallow like himself, but august and serene like a ruler. He uttered with a soldierly stutter the official compliment which he had learnt by heart. The President answered him : " I thank you in the name of the Republic and of our country which you loyally serve." At this, all the devotion to an absent prince which

General Cartier de Chalmot had stored up for twenty-five years welled forth from his heart towards the President, whose quiet face remained surprisingly immobile, and who spoke in a melancholy voice with no movement of cheek or lips, on which his black beard set a seal. On this waxen face, in these slow, honest eyes, on this feeble breast, across which blazed the broad red ribbon of his order, in the whole figure of this suffering automaton, the general perceived both the dignity of the leader, and the affliction of the ill-fated man who has never laughed. With his admiration there was mingled a strain of tenderness.

A year later he heard of the tragic end of this President for whose safety he would willingly have died, and whom he henceforth pictured in his thoughts as dark and stiff, like the flag rolled round its staff in the barracks and covered with its case.

From that time he had ignored the civil rulers of France. He cared to know nothing save of his military superiors, whom he obeyed with melancholy punctiliousness. Pained at the idea of answering the venerable Abbé de Lalonde by a refusal, he bethought himself for a moment, and then gave his reasons.

"A matter of principle. I never ask anything of the government. You agree with me, don't you? . . . For from the moment that one lays down a rule for oneself . . ."

The chaplain looked at him with an expression of

sadness that seemed as though thrown over his happy old face.

"Oh! how could I agree with you, general—I who beg of everybody? I am a hardened beggar. For God and the poor, I have pleaded with all the powers of the day, with King Louis Philippe's ministers, with those of the provisional government, with Napoleon III.'s ministers, with those of the *Ordre Moral* and those of the present Republic. They have all helped me to do some good. And since you know the Minister of Religion . . ."

At this moment a shrill voice called in the passage: "Poulot! Poulot!"

And a stout lady in a morning wrapper, her white hair crowned with hair-curlers, entered the room with a rush. It was Madame Cartier de Chalmot, who was calling the general to déjeuner.

She had already shaken her husband with imperious tenderness, and exclaimed once more: "Poulot!" before she became aware of the presence of the old priest crushed up against the door.

She apologised for her untidy dress. She had had so much to do this morning! Three daughters, two sons, an orphan nephew and her husband— seven children to look after!

"Ah! madame," said the abbé, "it is God himself who has sent you! You will be my providence."

"Your providence, monsieur l'abbé ! "

In her grey dressing-gown her figure revealed the ample dignity of classic motherhood. On her beaming moustachioed face shone a matronly pride ; her large gestures expressed at once the briskness of a housewife habituated to work and the ease of a woman accustomed to official deference. The general disappeared behind her. She was his house-hold goddess and his guardian angel, this Pauline who carried on her brave, energetic shoulders all the burden of this poverty-stricken, ostentatious house, who played the part of seamstress to the family, as well as cook, dressmaker, chambermaid, governess, apothecary, and even milliner with a frankly gaudy taste, and yet showed at big dinners and receptions an imperturbable good breeding, a commanding profile, and shoulders that were still beautiful. It was commonly said in the division that if the general became Minister of War, his wife would do the honours of the hôtel in the Boulevard Saint-Germain * in capital fashion.

The energy of the general's wife spread freely over into the outer world and flourished vigorously in pious and charitable works. Madame Cartier de Chalmot was lady patroness of three crêches and a dozen charities recommended by the Cardinal-Archbishop. Monseigneur Charlot showed a special

* Where the French War Office is situated.

predilection for this lady, and said to her sometimes, with his man-of-the-world smile : " You are
a general in the army of Christian charity." And,
being a professor of orthodoxy, Monseigneur Charlot
never failed to add : " And there is no charity outside the Christian charity ; for the Church alone is
in a position to solve the social problems whose
difficulties perplex the minds of all and cause special
anxiety to our paternal heart."

This was just what Madame Cartier de Chalmot
thought. She was lavishly, glaringly pious, and not
free from the rather loud magnificence that was
aptly accented by the sound of her voice and the
flowers in her hats. Her faith, voluminous and
decorative like the bosom which enshrined it, made
a splendid show in drawing-rooms. By the breadth
of her religious sentiments she had done much harm
to her husband. But neither of them paid any heed
to this. The general also believed in the Christian
creed, although this would not have prevented him
from having the Cardinal-Archbishop arrested on a
written order from the Minister of War. Yet he
was regarded with suspicion by the democracy.
And the *préfet*, M. Worms-Clavelin himself, though
little of a fanatic, regarded General Cartier de
Chalmot as a dangerous man. This was his wife's
fault. She was ambitious, but the soul of honour
and incapable of betraying her God.

"How can I be your providence, monsieur l'abbé ?"

And when she heard that the point at issue was the raising to the bishopric of Tourcoing of Abbé Lantaigne, a man of such noble, steadfast piety, she caught fire and showed her courage.

"Those are the bishops we want. M. Lantaigne ought to be nominated."

The old chaplain began to make use of this happy valiancy.

"Then, madame, induce the general to write to the Minister of Religion, who turns out to be his friend."

She shook the crown of curlers on her head vigorously.

"No, monsieur l'abbé. My husband will not write. It is useless to persist. He thinks that a soldier ought never to ask for anything. He is right. My father was of this opinion. You knew him, monsieur l'abbé, and you know that he was a fine man and a good soldier."

The old Army chaplain smote his forehead.

"Colonel de Balny ! Yes, of course, I knew him. He was a hero and a Christian."

General Cartier de Chalmot interposed :

"My father-in-law, Colonel de Balny, was chiefly commendable for having mastered in their entirety the regulations of 1829 on cavalry manœuvres. These regulations were so complicated that few officers mastered them in their completeness. They were afterwards withdrawn, and Colonel de Balny conceived such a disgust at this that it hastened his end. New regulations were imposed, possessing the unquestionable advantage of simplification. Yet I question whether the old state of things was not preferable. You must exact much from a cavalryman in order to get a little out of him. It is the same with the foot-soldier."

And the general began anxiously to manipulate his division of cards drawn up in the boxes.

Madame Cartier de Chalmot had heard these same words very often. She always made the same reply to them. Once more this time she said :

"Poulot ! how can you say that papa died of chagrin, when he fell down in an apoplectic fit at a review ? "

The old chaplain, by a crafty wile, brought the conversation back to the subject which interested him.

"Ah ! madame, your excellent father, Colonel de Balny, would have certainly appreciated the character of M. Lantaigne, and he would have offered up prayers that this priest might be raised to a bishopric."

"I also, monsieur l'abbé, will offer up prayers for that," answered the general's wife. "My husband cannot, ought not to make any application. But if you think that my intervention will be useful, I will drop a word to Monseigneur.   He doesn't terrify me at all, our Archbishop.

"Doubtless a word from your mouth . . ." murmured the old man. ". . . The ear of Monseigneur Charlot will be open to it."

The general's wife announced that she would be seeing the Archbishop at the inauguration of the Pain de Saint Antoine, of which she was president, and that there . . .

She interrupted herself :

"The cutlets ! . . . Excuse me, monsieur l'abbé . . ."

She rushed out on to the landing and shouted orders to the cook from the staircase. Then she reappeared in the room.

"And there I shall draw him aside, and beg him to speak to the nuncio in favour of M. Lantaigne. Is that the right way to go to work ? "

The old chaplain made as if to take her hands, yet without actually doing so.

" That's just the way, madame.   I am sure that the good Saint Anthony of Padua will be with you and will help you to persuade Monseigneur Charlot. He is a great saint. I mean Saint Anthony. . . . Ladies ought not to believe that he devotes himself exclusively to finding the jewels which they have lost. In heaven he has something better to do. To beg him for bread for the poor, that is assuredly far worthier. You have realised that, dear madame. The Pain de Saint Antoine is a fine work. I must inform myself more fully about it. But I shall take good care not to breathe a word of it to my good sisters."

He was referring to the Dames du Salut, to whom he was chaplain.

" They have already too many undertakings. They are excellent sisters, but too much absorbed in trifling duties, and far too petty, the poor ladies."

He sighed, recalling the time when he was a regimental chaplain, the tragic days of the war, when he accompanied the wounded stretched out on an ambulance litter and gave them a drop of brandy. For it was by doles of tobacco and spirits that he was in the habit of carrying on his apostolic labours. He again gave way to his love of talking about the fighting round Metz and told some anecdotes. He had several concerning a certain sapper, a native of Lorraine called Larmoise, a man full of resources.

" I did not tell you, general, how this great devil of a sapper used to bring me a bag of potatoes every morning. One day I asked him where he picked them up. Says he : ' In the enemy's lines.' ' You villain,' I say to him. Thereupon he explains to me how he has found some fellow-countrymen among the German guards. ' Fellow-countrymen ? ' ' Yes, fellow-countrymen, fellows from home. We are only separated by the frontier. We embraced one another, we talked about our relatives and friends. And they said to me : "You can take as many potatoes as you like." ' "

And the chaplain added :

"This simple incident made me feel better than any reasoning how cruel and unjust war is."

"Yes," said the general, "these annoying intimacies occasionally occur at the points of contact of two armies. They must be sternly repressed, having due regard, of course, to the circumstances."

VII

N the promenade along the ramparts that evening Abbé Lantaigne, head of the high seminary, fell in with M. Bergeret, a professor of literature who was considered a man of remarkable, but eccentric character. M. Lantaigne forgave him his scepticism and chatted with him willingly, whenever he met him under the elm-trees on the Mall. On his side, M. Bergeret had no objection to studying the mind of an intelligent priest. They both knew that their conversations on a seat in the promenade were equally displeasing to the dean of the Faculty and to the Archbishop. But Abbé Lantaigne knew nothing about worldly prudence, and M. Bergeret, very weary, discouraged, and disillusioned, had given up caring for fruitless considerations of policy.

Sceptical within the bounds of decorum and good taste, the assiduous devotions of his wife and the endless catechisms of his daughters had resulted in his being impeached of clericalism in the ministerial

bureaux, whilst certain speeches that had been attributed to him were used against him, both by professing Catholics and professional patriots. Foiled in his
ambitions, he still meant to live in his own way, and
having failed to learn how to please, tried discreetly
to displease.

On this peaceful and radiant evening M. Bergeret,
seeing the head of the high seminary coming along
his usual road, advanced several paces to meet the
priest and joined him under the first elm-trees on
the Mall.

"To me the place is happy where I meet you,"
said Abbé Lantaigne, who loved, before a university
man, to air his harmless literary affectations.

In a few very vague phrases they made a mutual
confession of the great pity aroused in them both
by the world in which they lived. It was Abbé
Lantaigne alone who deplored the decay of this
ancient city, so rich, during the Middle Ages, in
knowledge and thought, and now subject to a few
petty tradesmen and freemasons. In frank opposition
to this, M. Bergeret said :

"In days gone by men were just what they are
now ; that is to say, moderately good and moderately
bad."

"Not so !" answered M. Lantaigne. "Men were
vigorous in character and strong in doctrine when
Raymond the Great, surnamed the balsamic doctor,

taught in this town the epitome of human knowledge."

The professor and the priest sat down on a stone
bench where two old men, pale-faced and decrepit,
were already sitting without saying a word. In front
of this bench, green meadows, wreathed in light
mist, stretched gently downwards to the poplars that
fringed the river.

"Monsieur l'abbé," said the professor, "I have,
like everybody else, turned over the pages of the
Hortus and the *Thesaurus* of Raymond the Great in
the municipal library. Moreover, I have read the
new book that Abbé Cazeaux has devoted to the
balsamic doctor. Now, what struck me in that
book . . ."

"Abbé Cazeaux is one of my pupils," interrupted M. Lantaigne. "His book on Raymond
the Great is based on facts, which is praiseworthy;
it is founded on theology, which is still more praiseworthy and rare, for theology is lost in this decadent
France, which was the greatest of the nations as long
as she was the most theological."

"This book of M. Cazeaux's," answered M.
Bergeret, "appeared to me to be interesting from
several points of view. For want of a knowledge of
theology I lost myself in it more than once. Yet
I fancied I could see in it that the blessed Raymond, rigidly orthodox monk as he was, claimed for

the teacher the right of professing two contradictory
opinions on the same subject, the one theological
and in accordance with revelation, the other purely
human and based on experience or reason.   The
balsamic doctor, whose statue adorns so sternly
the courtyard of the Archbishop's palace, maintained,
according to what I have been able to understand,
that one and the same man may deny, as an observer
or as a disputant, the truths which, as a Christian,
he believes and confesses.   And it seemed to me
that your pupil, M. Cazeaux, approved of a system
so strange."

Abbé Lantaigne, quite animated by what he had
just heard, drew his red silk handkerchief from his
pocket, unfurled it like a flag, and with flushed face
and mouth wide open flung himself fearlessly on the
challenge thrown down.

" Monsieur Bergeret, as to whether one can have,
on the same subject, two distinct opinions, the one
theological and of divine origin, the other purely
rational or experimental and of human origin, that is
a question which I answer in the affirmative.   And
I am going to prove to you the truth of this
apparent contradiction by a most common instance.
When, seated in your study, before your table
loaded with books and papers, you exclaim, ' It is
incredible !   I have just this moment put my paper-
knife on this table and now I do not see it there.

I see it, I'm sure I see it, and yet I no longer see it,'
when you think in this way, Monsieur Bergeret,
you have two contradictory opinions with respect to
the same object, one that your paper-knife is on the
table because it ought to be there : that opinion is
based on reason ; the other that your paper-knife
is not on the table, because you do not see it there :
that opinion is based on experience. There you
have two irreconcilable opinions on the same subject.
And they are simultaneous. You affirm at the same
time both the presence and the absence of the paper-
knife. You exclaim, 'It is there, I am sure of it,'
at the very moment you are proving it is not there."

And, having finished his demonstration, Abbé
Lantaigne waved his chequered, snuff-besprinkled silk
handkerchief, like the flaming banner of scholasticism.

But the professor of literature was not convinced.
He had no difficulty in showing the emptiness of
this sophism. He replied quite gently in the rather
weak voice that he habitually husbanded, that, in
looking for his paper-knife, he experienced fear and
hope, by turns and not simultaneously, the result of
an uncertainty which could not last ; for it ended by
his making sure whether the knife was on the table
or not.

"There is nothing, monsieur l'abbé," added he,
"nothing in this instance of the boxwood knife that
is applicable to the contradictory judgment which the

blessed Raymond, or M. Cazeaux, or you yourself, might form on such or such a fact recorded in the Bible, when you state that it is at the same time both true and false.   Allow me, in my turn, to give you an instance.   I choose,—not, of course, in order to ensnare you, but because this incident comes of its own accord into my mind,—I choose the story of Joshua causing the sun to stand still. . . ."

M. Bergeret passed his tongue over his lips and smiled.   For in truth he was, in the secret places of his soul, a Voltairean :

" . . . Joshua causing the sun to stand still. Will you tell me, straight out, monsieur l'abbé, that Joshua made the sun stand still and did not make it stand still ? "

The head of the high seminary had by no means an air of embarrassment.   Splendid controversialist as he was, he turned to his opponent with flashing eyes and heaving breast.

" After every reservation has been expressly made with respect to the true interpretation, both literal and spiritual, of the passage in Judges which you attack and against which so many unbelievers have blindly dashed themselves before you, I will reply to you fearlessly.   Yes, I have two distinct opinions as to the interpretation of this miracle.   I believe as a natural philosopher, for reasons drawn from physics, that is to say, from observation, that the earth turns round a motionless sun. And as a theologian I believe that Joshua caused the sun to stand still. There is here a contradiction. But this contradiction is not irreconcilable. I will prove it to you at once. For the idea which we form of the sun is purely human ; it only concerns man and could not be applicable to God. For man, the sun does not turn round the earth. I grant it, and I am willing to decide in favour of Copernicus. But I will not go so far as to force God to become a Copernican like myself, and I shall not inquire whether, for God, the sun turns or does not turn round the earth. To speak truly, I had no need of the text of Judges in order to know that our human astronomy is not the astronomy of God. Speculations as to time, number and space do not embrace infinity, and it is a mad idea to wish to entangle the Holy Spirit in a physical or mathematical difficulty."

"Then," asked the professor, "you admit that, even in mathematics, it is permissible to have two contradictory opinions, the one human, the other divine ? "

"I will not risk being reduced to that extremity," answered Abbé Lantaigne. "There is in mathematics an exactitude which practically reconciles it with absolute truth. Numbers, on the contrary, are only dangerous because the reason, being tempted to seek in them for its own principle, runs the risk of

F

going so far astray as to see nothing in the universe save a system of numbers. This error has been condemned by the Church. Yet I will answer you boldly that human mathematics are not divine mathematics. Doubtless, however, it would not be possible for one to contradict the other, and I prefer to believe that you do not wish to make me say that for God three and three can make nine. But we do not know all the properties of numbers, and God does.

" I hear that there are priests, regarded as eminent, who maintain that science ought to agree with theology. I detest this impertinence, I will say this impiety, for there is a certain impiety in making the immutable and absolute truth walk in harmony with that imperfect and provisional truth which is called science. This madness of assimilating reality to appearance, the body to the soul, has produced a multitude of miserable, baneful opinions through which the apologists of this period have allowed their foolhardy feebleness to be seen. One, a distinguished member of the Society of Jesus, admits the plurality of inhabited worlds ; he allows that intelligent beings may inhabit Mars and Venus, provided that to the earth there be reserved the privilege of the Cross, by which it again becomes unique and peculiar in the Creation. The other, a man who not without some merit occupied in the

Sorbonne the chair of theology which has since been abolished, grants that the geologist can trace the vestiges of preadamites and reduces the Genesis of the Bible to the organisation of one province of the universe for the sojourn of Adam and his seed. O dull folly ! O pitiable boldness ! O ancient novelties, already condemned a hundred times ! O violation of sacred unity ! How much better, like Raymond the Great and his historian, to proclaim that science and religion ought no more to be confused with each other than the relative and the absolute, the finite and the infinite, the darkness and the light !"

"Monsieur l'abbé," said the professor, "you despise science."

The priest shook his head.

"Not so, Monsieur Bergeret, not so ! I hold, on the contrary, according to the example of Saint Thomas Aquinas and all the great doctors, that science and philosophy ought to be held in high esteem in the schools.

"One does not despise science without despising reason ; one does not despise reason without despising man ; one does not despise man without insulting God. The rash scepticism which lays the blame on human reason is the first step towards that criminal scepticism that defies the divine mysteries. I value science as a gift which comes to us from God.

But if God has given us science, he has not given us *His* science. His geometry is not ours. Ours speculates on one plane or in space; His works in infinitude. He has not deceived us: that is why I consider that there is a true human science. He has not taught us all: that is why I declare the powerlessness of this science, even though true, to agree with the truth of truths. And this discrepancy, every time that it occurs between the two, I see without fear: it proves nothing, neither against heaven, nor earth."

M. Bergeret confessed that this system seemed to him as clever as it was bold, and ultimately consonant with the interests of the faith.

"But," added he, "it is not our Archbishop's doctrine. In his pastoral letters, Monseigneur Charlot speaks voluntarily of the truths of religion being confirmed by the discoveries of science, and especially by the experiments of M. Pasteur."

"Oh!" answered Abbé Lantaigne in a nasal voice that hissed with scorn, "His Eminence observes, in philosophy at least, the vow of evangelical poverty."

At the moment when this phrase was lashing the air beneath the quincunxes, a corpulent great-coat, capped by a wide clerical hat, passed in front of the bench.

"Speak lower, monsieur l'abbé," said the professor; "Abbé Guitrel hears you."

VIII

*LE PRÉFET* WORMS-CLAVELIN was chatting with Abbé Guitrel in the shop of Rondonneau junior, goldsmith and jeweller. He leant back in an arm-chair and crossed his legs so that the sole of one of his boots stuck up towards the placid old man's chin.

"Monsieur l'abbé, it is useless for you to speak : you are an enlightened priest ; you see in religion a collection of moral precepts, a necessary discipline, and not a set of antiquated dogmas, of mysteries whose absurdity is only too little mysterious."

As a priest, M. Guitrel had excellent rules of conduct. One of these rules was to avoid scandal and to hold his tongue, rather than expose the truth to the mockery of unbelievers. And, as this precaution agreed with the bent of his character, he observed it scrupulously. But M. *le préfet* Worms-Clavelin was lacking in discretion. His vast, fleshy nose, his thick lips, seemed like a powerful apparatus of suction and absorption, whilst his receding fore-

head, above his great pale eyes, betrayed his opposition to all moral delicacy.   He persisted, marshalled
against Christian dogmas the arguments of the
masonic lodges and the literary cafés, and concluded
by saying that it was impossible for an intelligent
man to believe a word of the Catechism.   Then,
bringing down his fat, beringed hand on the priest's
shoulder, he said :

"You don't answer, my dear abbé ; you are of
my opinion."

M. Guitrel, in some sort a martyr, was forced
to confess his faith.

"Pardon me, monsieur *le préfet;* that little
book, the Catechism, which it is the fashion to
despise in certain quarters, contains more truths than
the great treatises on philosophy which make such
a vast noise in the world.   The Catechism unites
the most learned metaphysics with the most effective
simplicity.   This appreciation is not mine ; it is that
of an eminent philosopher, M. Jules Simon, who
ranks the Catechism above Plato's *Timæus.*"

The *préfet* dared not contradict the opinion of an
ex-minister.   He remembered at the same time that
his official superior, the present Secretary of State
for the Home Department, was a Protestant.   He
said : "As an official I respect all religions equally,
Protestantism as well as Catholicism.   As a man, I
am a freethinker, and if I had any preference as to

dogma, let me tell you, monsieur l'abbé, that it would be in favour of the Reformed Party."

M. Guitrel replied in an unctuous voice : " There are, doubtless, among Protestants, many persons eminently estimable from the point of view of morals, and I dare say many exemplary persons, if they are judged from the world's standpoint. But the so-called reformed Church is but a limb hacked from the Catholic Church, and the place of the wound still bleeds."

Indifferent to this powerful phrase, borrowed from Bossuet, M. *le préfet* drew from his case a big cigar, lighted it, and holding out the case to the priest :

" Will you accept a cigar, monsieur l'abbé ? "

Being densely ignorant of ecclesiastical discipline, and believing that tobacco-smoking was forbidden to the clergy, he offered a cigar to M. Guitrel in order to make him look awkward or to lead him astray. In his ignorance he believed that by this offer he was leading a wearer of the cassock into sin, making him fall into disobedience, perhaps into sacrilege, and almost into apostasy. But M. Guitrel placidly took the cigar, slipped it carefully into the pocket of his great-coat, and said urbanely that he would smoke it after supper in his room.

Thus M. *le préfet* Worms-Clavelin and Abbé Guitrel, professor of sacred rhetoric at the high seminary, conversed in the goldsmith's office. Near

them, Rondonneau junior, contractor to the Archbishop, who also worked for the prefecture, listened
to the conversation discreetly, without taking part in
it.   He was preparing his mail, and his bald pate
came and went among his account-books and the
samples of commercial jewellery heaped up on the
table.

With a brusque movement M. *le préfet* stood upright, pushed Abbé Guitrel to the other end of the
room, into the recess of the window, and whispered
in his ear :

" My dear Guitrel, you know that the bishopric of
Tourcoing is vacant."

" I have in fact," answered the priest, " learnt of
the death of Monseigneur Duclou.   It is a great loss
for the Church of France.   Monseigneur Duclou's
merits were only equalled by his modesty.   He
excelled in preaching.   His pastoral addresses are
models of hortatory eloquence.   Shall I dare to recall
to mind that I knew him in Orleans, at the time when
he was still Abbé Duclou, the revered curé of Saint-
Euverte, and that at that time he deigned to honour
me with his gracious friendship ?   The news of his
premature death was particularly distressing to me."

He was silent, letting his lips droop in sign of
grief.

" It's not a question of that," said the *préfet*.   " He
is dead ; it is a question of filling his place."

M. Guitrel's face changed.   Now, screwing up his little eyes till they were quite round, he looked like a rat who sees bacon in the larder.

"You must know, my dear Guitrel," continued the *préfet*, "that this business has nothing whatever to do with me.   It is not I who appoint the bishops. I am not the keeper of the seals, nor the nuncio, nor the Pope.   God be thanked!"

And he began to laugh.

"By the bye, on what terms do you stand with the nuncio?"

"The nuncio, monsieur *le préfet*, looks upon me with friendliness, as a humble and dutiful servant of the Holy Father.   But I do not flatter myself that he especially heeds me, in the humble station in which I have been placed and where I am content to remain."

"My dear abbé, if I speak to you about this affair—quite between ourselves, isn't it?—it is because there is a question of sending a priest from my county town to Tourcoing.   I hear on good authority that the name of Abbé Lantaigne, head of the high seminary, is being brought forward, and it is not impossible that I may be asked to supply confidential information about the candidate.   He is your ecclesiastical superior.   What do you think of him?"

M. Guitrel answered, with downcast eyes :

"It is certain that Abbé Lantaigne would bring to the episcopal see once sanctified by the apostle Loup

both eminent piety and the precious gifts of eloquence. His Lenten sermons preached at Saint-
Exupère have been justly admired for their logical
arrangement of ideas and power of expression, and it
is commonly recognised that some of the sermons
would fall in no respect short of perfection, if there
were present in them that unction, that perfumed and
consecrated oil, if I may dare so to call it, which alone
penetrates the heart.

"The curé of Saint-Exupère took pleasure in
being the first to declare that M. Lantaigne, in speaking the word from the pulpit of the most venerable
church in the diocese, had deserved well of the great
apostle of the Gauls who laid the first stone of it, by
reason of an ardour and a zeal whose very excesses
were excused by their benevolent origin. He only
deplored the orator's excursions into the domain of
contemporary history. For it must needs be confessed that M. Lantaigne has no fear of walking on
embers that are still burning. M. Lantaigne is
distinguished by piety, learning and talent. What a
pity that a priest worthy of being raised to the highest
positions in the Church should believe it to be his duty
to proclaim a devotion, doubtless praiseworthy in
principle, but reckless in its results, to an exiled
family from whom he has received favours. He takes
pleasure in showing a copy of the *Imitation de Jésus-
Christ*, bound in purple and gold, which was given

to him by the Comtesse de Paris, and he displays far too freely the extent of his gratitude and fidelity. And what a misfortune that an arrogance, excusable perhaps in such lofty talent, should lead him even to the lengths of speaking publicly under the quincunxes about the Cardinal-Archbishop in terms which I dare not repeat ! Alas ! failing my voice, all the trees on the Mall would re-utter these words that fell from the mouth of M. Lantaigne, in the presence of M. Bergeret, professor of literature : 'In brain alone, His Eminence observes the evangelical vow of poverty !' Such sayings are habitual with him, and was he not heard to say at the last ordination, when His Eminence advanced clothed in those pontifical ornaments which he bears with so much dignity, notwithstanding his short stature : 'Golden cross, wooden bishop'? Most unseasonably he thus censured the magnificence with which Monseigneur Charlot delights to celebrate the offices as well as to regulate the ordering of his official banquets, and especially the dinner which he gave to the general in command of the new army-corps, and to which you were invited, Monsieur le préfet. And in particular any better agreement between the prefecture and the archbishopric offends Abbé Lantaigne, who is far too inclined, unfortunately, to prolong the painful misunderstandings from which Church and State suffer equally, in scorn

of the precepts of St. Paul and the teaching of His
Holiness Leo XIII."

The *préfet* opened his mouth quite wide, being in
the habit of listening with it.   He burst out :

"This Lantaigne is steeped in the most detestable
spirit of clericalism !   He owes me a grudge ?   What
has he got against me ?   Am I not tolerant and
liberal enough ?   Did I not shut my eyes when on
all sides the monks and nuns re-entered the con-
vents, the schools ?   For if we vigorously uphold
the essential laws of the Republic, we hardly enforce
them.   But priests are incorrigible.   You are all the
same.   You cry out that you are being oppressed as
soon as you yourself are not oppressing.   And what
does he say about me, this Lantaigne of yours ?"

"Nothing definite can be set forth against the
administration of M. *le préfet* Worms-Clavelin, but
an uncompromising soul like M. Lantaigne never
forgives either your association with freemasonry or
your Jewish origin."

The *préfet* shook the ash from his cigar.   "The
Jews are no friends of mine.   I have no ties in
the Jewish world.   But be tranquil, my dear abbé,
I give you my word that M. Lantaigne shall not be
bishop of Tourcoing.   I have enough influence in
the bureaux to checkmate him. . . . Just listen to
me, Guitrel : I had no money when I started out in
life.   I made connections for myself.   Connections

are worth nearly as much as wealth. I have many
and good ones. I shall be on the watch to see that
Abbé Lantaigne cuts his own throat in the bureaux.
Besides, my wife has a candidate for the bishopric
of Tourcoing. And that candidate is you, Guitrel."

At this word, Abbé Guitrel cast down his eyes
and flung up his arms.

" I, sit in the seat sanctified by the blessed Loup
and by so many pious apostles of Northern Gaul !
Can such a thought have occurred to Madame
Worms-Clavelin ? "

" My dear Guitrel, she wishes that you should
wear the mitre. And I assure you she is powerful
enough to create a bishop. For my part, I shall not
be sorry to give a Republican bishop to the Republic.
That's understood, my dear Guitrel ; you look after
the Archbishop and the nuncio ; my wife and I
will set the bureaux in motion."

And M. Guitrel murmured with clasped hands :

" The ancient and venerable see of Tourcoing ! "

" A third-class bishopric, a mere hole, my dear
abbé. But one must make a beginning. Why !
do you know where I started my career in official
life ? At Céret ! I was *sous-préfet* of Céret, in the
Pyrénées-Orientales ! Would any one credit it ?
. . . But I am wasting my time gossiping . . .
Good evening, Monseigneur."

The *préfet* held out his hand to the priest. And

M. Guitrel went off along the winding street of the Tintelleries, humbly and with shoulders bent, yet planning cunning measures and promising himself, on the day when he wore the mitre and grasped the crozier, to resist the civil Government, like a prince of the Church, to fight the freemasons and to hurl anathemas at the principles of freethought, the Republic, and the Revolution.

IX

N article in *le Libéral* informed the town of . . . that it possessed a prophetess. This was Mademoiselle Claude Deniseau, daughter of a man who kept a registry for country servants. Up to the age of seventeen Mademoiselle Deniseau had not revealed to the closest observer any abnormality of mind or body. She was a fair, fat, short girl, neither pretty nor ugly, but pleasant and of a lively disposition. "She had received," said *le Libéral*, "a good middle-class education, and she was religious without bigotry." At the beginning of her eighteenth year, on the 3rd of February, 189–, at six o'clock in the evening, being engaged in laying the cloth on the table in the dining-room, she thought she heard her mother's voice saying, "Claudine, go to your room." She went there and between the bed and the door she perceived a bright light, and heard a voice which spoke from the light, saying : "Claudine, this country must do penance, for that will ward off great

misfortunes. I am Saint Radegonde, Queen of France." Mademoiselle Deniseau then descried in the splendour a luminous and, as it were, transparent face that wore a crown of gold and gems.

After that Saint Radegonde came every day to converse with Mademoiselle Deniseau, to whom she revealed secrets and made prophecies. She had foretold the frosts that blighted the vine in blossom, and revealed that M. Rieu, curé of Sainte-Agnès, would not see the Easter festival. The venerable M. Rieu actually died on Holy Thursday. For the Republic and for France she never ceased to foretell terrible disasters close at hand—fires, floods, massacres. But God, wearied of chastising a faithless people, would at last, under a king, bring back peace and prosperity to it. The saint diagnosed and cured diseases. Under her inspiration, Mademoiselle Deniseau had told Jobelin, the road-mender, of an ointment which had cured him of an anchylosis of the knee. Jobelin had been able to resume his work again.

These marvels attracted a crowd of inquirers to the flat inhabited by the Deniseau family in the Place Saint-Exupère, above the tramway office. The young girl was studied by ecclesiastics, retired officers, and doctors of medicine. They believed that they noticed, when she was repeating the words of Saint Radegonde, that her voice became deeper,

her expression sterner, and that her limbs became
rigid.   They also noticed that she used expressions
which are not customary with young girls, and that
her words could be explained by no natural means.

M. *le préfet* Worms-Clavelin, at first indifferent and
scoffing, soon followed the extraordinary success of
the prophetess with anxiety, for she announced the
end of the Republic and the return of France to a
Christian monarchy.

M. Worms-Clavelin had entered office at the time
of the scandals at the Élysée under President Grévy.
Since then he had participated in those cases of
corruption that are endlessly being hushed up and as
constantly revived to the great detriment of Parliament and the public authority.   And this spectacle,
which seemed natural to him, had ingrafted in his
mind a profound feeling of laxity, which spread from
him to all his subordinates.   A senator and two
deputies from his department were being threatened
with legal proceedings.   The most influential members of the party, engineers and financiers, were either
in prison or in hiding.   Under these circumstances,
satisfied that the people were attached to the republican
rule, he expected from them neither enthusiasm nor
deference, which seemed to him but old-fashioned
qualities and the empty symbols of a vanished age.
Events had enlarged his naturally limited intelligence.
The vast irony of things had passed into his soul,

G

making it easy-going, mocking, indifferent.   Having
recognised, moreover, that the electoral committees
constituted the only real authority that still subsisted
in the department, he obeyed them with a semblance
of zeal and with secret opposition.   If he executed
their orders, it was not without a considerable modifi-
cation of their rigour.   In a word, from opportunist
he had become liberal and progressive.   He willingly
allowed liberty of speech and action.   But he was too
wise to allow any unbearable excesses, and, like a
conscientious official, he took good care that the
government should not receive any glaring insult, and
that the ministers should peaceably enjoy that common
attitude of indifference which, by gaining over their
friends as well as their enemies, ensured at the same
time both their power and their repose.

It pleased him that the governmental papers and
the opposition ones, both being compromised by
financial transactions, should be utterly discredited,
alike as to their praise and their blame.   The socialist
sheet, being the only independent one, was also the
only violent one.   But it was very poor ; and the fear
which it inspired drove people back towards the
government.   Thus M. *le préfet* Worms-Clavelin
was entirely sincere when he informed the Home
Secretary that the political situation was excellent in
his department.   And here was the prophetess of
the Place Saint-Exupère destroying the harmony of

this happy state. Under the direction of Saint Radegonde, she announced the fall of the ministry, the dissolution of Parliament, the resignation of the President of the Republic, and the collapse of a discredited government. She was much more violent than *le Libéral* and far more influential. For *le Libéral* drew but few, while the whole town thronged around Mademoiselle Deniseau. The clergy, the large landowners, the nobility, the clerical press, hung upon her and drank in her words. Saint Radegonde rallied the defeated enemies of the Republic and brought together the " Conservatives." A harmless rally, but inconvenient. M. Worms-Clavelin was especially afraid lest a Paris paper should noise the affair about. " It would then assume," said he to himself, " the proportions of a scandal and would expose me to a reprimand from the minister." He resolved to look for the quietest way of silencing Mademoiselle Deniseau, and first began to make inquiries as to the character of her relations.

Her father's family was not much respected in the town. The Deniseaux were people of no position. Mademoiselle Claude's father kept a registry office, the reputation of which was neither better nor worse than that of other registries. Masters and servants complained of it, but still made use of it. In 1871 Deniseau had had the Commune proclaimed in the Place Saint-Exupère. Somewhat later, upon the expulsion of three Dominicans at the point of the sword, he had offered resistance to the gendarmes, and had got himself arrested. Next he had stood at municipal elections as a socialist, and had only obtained a very small number of votes. He was hot-headed and weak-minded, but believed to be honest.

The mother was a Nadal. The Nadals, in a better position than the Deniseaux, were small agricultural proprietors, all much respected. One of the Nadals, an aunt to Mademoiselle Claude, being subject to hallucinations, had been shut up in an asylum for some years. The Nadals were religious and had clerical connections. M. Worms-Clavelin could learn nothing more about them.

One morning he had a conversation on this subject with his private secretary, M. Lacarelle, who belonged to an old family in the neighbourhood and knew the department well.

"My dear Lacarelle, we must put an end to this madness. For it is plain that Mademoiselle Deniseau is mad."

Lacarelle replied gravely, not without the kind of arrogance inseparable from his long fair moustaches.

"Monsieur *le préfet*, opinions are divided with respect to this, and many people believe that Mademoiselle Deniseau is perfectly sane."

"After all, Lacarelle, you do not believe that

Saint Radegonde comes every morning to chat with her and to drag the head of the State, along with the Government, down into the mire."

But Lacarelle was of opinion that there had been exaggeration, that ill-disposed persons were making the most of an extraordinary manifestation. It really was extraordinary that Mademoiselle Deniseau should prescribe sovereign remedies for incurable diseases ; she had cured Jobelin, the road-mender, and an old bailiff called Favru. That was not all. She foretold events that fell out as she had said.

"I can vouch for one fact, monsieur *le préfet*. Last week Mademoiselle Deniseau said: 'There is a treasure hidden in a field called Faifeu, at Noiselles.' They dug at the place described and discovered a great slab of stone which blocked the entrance of an underground passage."

"But, still," cried the *préfet*, "you cannot maintain that Saint Radegonde . . ."

He stopped, thoughtful and questioning. He was profoundly ignorant of the saintly legends of Christian Gaul and of the national antiquities of France. But at school he had studied text-books of history. He was struggling to recall his boyish recollections.

"Saint Radegonde was the mother of Saint Louis ? "

M. Lacarelle, who knew more history, only hesitated a moment.

"No," said he, "the mother of Saint Louis was Blanche of Castille.   Saint Radegonde was an earlier queen."

"Well, she cannot be allowed to perform her conjuring tricks in the county town.   And you, my dear Lacarelle, you ought to make her father understand—this Deniseau, I mean to say—that he has nothing to do but to give a good flogging to his daughter and put her under lock and key."

Lacarelle smoothed his Gallic moustaches.

"Monsieur *le préfet*, I advise you to go and see this Deniseau girl.   She is interesting.   She will give you a private sitting quite to yourself."

"You can't mean it, Lacarelle!   Fancy my going to be instructed by a little hussy that my Government is on the point of collapse!"

M. *le préfet* Worms-Clavelin was not credulous. He only thought of religion from a political point of view.   He had inherited no creed from his parents, who were aliens to every superstition, as they were to every land.   His soul had sucked none of the nourishment of the past from any soil.   He remained empty, colourless, unfettered.   Through metaphysical incompetency and the instinctive feeling for action and acquisition, he clung to tangible truth, and in all good faith believed himself to be a positivist. Having but lately drunk his bocks in the cafés at Montmartre in the company of chemists with political opinions, he still preserved a blind trustfulness in scientific methods, which he in his turn extolled in the lodges to the leading spirits among the freemasons. He enjoyed embellishing his political intrigues and administrative expedients with the fair appearance of sociological experiment. And the more useful science was to him the better he appreciated it. " I profess," said he in all sincerity, " that unquestioning faith in facts which constitutes the scientist, the sociologist." And it was just because he only believed in facts and because he professed the creed of positivism that the affair of the Sibyl began to worry him.

His private secretary, M. Lacarelle, had said to him : " This young woman has cured a road-mender and a bailiff. These are facts. She has pointed out the place where they would discover a treasure, and they really found in that place a trap-door to the opening of a subterranean passage. That is a fact. She foretold the failure of the vines. That is a fact."

M. *le préfet* Worms-Clavelin had the instinct of mockery and a sense of humour, but this word *fact* exercised a spell over his mind ; and it occurred vaguely to his memory that doctors like Charcot had made observations in the hospitals on sick

people gifted with extraordinary powers. He remembered certain curious phenomena of hysteria
and cases of second sight. He wondered whether
Mademoiselle Deniseau were not a sufficiently
interesting hysteric patient for her to be handed
over to the experts in mental cases, which would rid
the town of her.

He thought :

" I might give an official order for the consignment
of this girl to an asylum, as in the case of any person
whose mental derangement forms a danger to public
order and personal safety ; but the enemies of the
government would squeal like polecats, and I can
already hear lawyer Lerond charging me with unlawful committal. The plot must be unravelled, if
the clericals of the county town have concocted one.
For it is not to be endured that Mademoiselle
Deniseau should declare every day, as the mouth-
piece of Saint Radegonde, that the Republic is sink-
ing into the mire. I grant that some regrettable
deeds have been done. Certain partial changes will
force themselves on us, especially in national representation, but, thank God, the government is still
strong enough for me to support it."

X

BBÉ LANTAIGNE, principal of the high seminary, and M. Bergeret, professor of literature, were seated in conversation on a bench on the Mall, according to their custom in summer. On every subject they were opposed in opinion; never were two men more different in mind and character. But they were the only people in the town who took an interest in general ideas. This fellow-feeling united them. While philosophising beneath the quincunxes when the weather was fine, they consoled each other, one for the loneliness of celibacy, the other for the vexations of domestic life; both for their professional cares and for the unpopularity each alike shared.

On this particular day they could see from the bench where they sat the monument of Jeanne d'Arc still shrouded in wrappings. The Maid having once slept a night in the town, at the house of an honest dame called la Gausse, in 189– the municipality, with the concurrence of the State, had caused a monument to be raised to commemorate this stay. This monument, the work of two artists, the one a sculptor and the other an architect, both natives of the district, displayed the Maid fully armed, standing, meditative, on a high pedestal.

The date of the unveiling was fixed for the following Sunday. The Minister of Education was expected, and it was reckoned that there would be a lavish distribution of crosses of honour and academic decorations. The townsfolk thronged the Mall to gaze at the linen which covered the bronze figure and the stone pedestal. Outsiders installed themselves on the ramparts. On the booths set up under the quincunxes the refreshment-sellers were nailing up bands of calico bearing the legends : *Véritable bière Jeanne d'Arc.—Café de la Pucelle.*

At sight of this, M. Bergeret remarked that one ought to rejoice in this concourse of citizens assembled to pay honour to the liberator of Orleans.

"The archivist of the department, M. Mazure," added he, "stands out from the crowd. He has written a memoir to prove that the famous historical tapestry, representing the meeting at Chinon, was not made about 1430 in Germany, as was believed, but that it came at that period from some studio of Flemish France. He submitted the conclusions of his memoir to M. *le préfet* Worms-Clavelin, who

called them eminently patriotic and approved of
them. He expressed a hope that he would see the
author of this discovery receiving the insignia of an
officer of the Academy beneath Jeanne's statue. It
is also rumoured that in his speech at the unveiling
M. *le préfet* will say, with his eyes turned towards
the Vosges, that Jeanne was a daughter of Alsace-
Lorraine."

Abbé Lantaigne, caring but little for a joke, made
no reply and kept a grave face. In principle he
regarded these celebrations in honour of Jeanne
d'Arc as praiseworthy. Two years before he had
himself pronounced at Saint-Exupère a panegyric
on the Maid, and had declared her the type of
the good Frenchwoman and the good Christian.
He found no subject for jest in a solemnity which
was a glorification of faith and country. As a
patriot and a Christian, he only regretted that the
bishop and his clergy would not take the first place
in it.

"The thing," said he, "that ensures the continuity
of the French nation, is neither kings nor presidents
of the Republic, neither provincial governors nor
préfets, neither officers of the crown nor officials of
the present government; it is the episcopacy which,
from the first apostles to the Gauls down to the
present day, has continued, without break, change,
or diminution, and forms, so to say, the solid web

of the history of France.   The power of the bishops is spiritual and stable.   The power of the kings, legitimate but transitory, is decrepit from its birth. On its continuance that of the nation does not depend.   The nation is a spiritual conception inseparable from the moral and religious idea.   But, although absent in the body from the celebrations that are being arranged for here, the clergy will be present at them in spirit and in truth.   Jeanne d'Arc is ours, and it is vain for unbelievers to try and steal her from us."

M. BERGERET: "It is, however, very natural that this simple girl, having become a symbol of patriotism, should be claimed by all patriots."

M. LANTAIGNE: "I cannot imagine—I have told you so before—nationality without religion.   Every duty comes from God, the duty of the citizen no less than that of others.   If God be ignored the call of duty is stilled.   If it is a right and a duty to defend one's native land against the foreigner, it is not in virtue of any pretended rights of man which never existed, but in conformity with the will of God.   This conformity appears in the stories of Jael and Judith.   It shines clearly in the book of the Maccabees.   It can be read in the deeds of the Maid."

M. BERGERET: "Then you believe, monsieur l'abbé, that Jeanne d'Arc received her mission from God

Himself? That will land you in numberless difficulties. I will only submit to you one of these,
because it is inherent in the nature of your beliefs.
It relates to the voices and apparitions which mani-
fested themselves to the peasant of Domremy.
Those who grant that Saint Catherine really appeared
to Jacquot d'Arc's daughter, in company with Saint
Michael and Saint Marguerite, will find themselves,
I fancy, much embarrassed when it has been proved
to them that this Saint Catherine of Alexandria never
existed, and that her history is in reality only a
rather poor Greek romance. Now this fact was
proved as early as the seventeenth century, not by
the freethinkers of the period, but by a learned
doctor of the Sorbonne, Jean de Launoy, a man of
piety and good life. The judicious Tillemont,
although so submissive to the Church, rejected the
biography of Saint Catherine as an absurd fable. Is
not that a difficulty, monsieur l'abbé, for those who
believe that the Voices of Jeanne d'Arc came from
Heaven?"

M. LANTAIGNE : "The martyrology, monsieur,
worthy of all reverence as it is, is not an article of
faith ; and it is permissible, in imitation of Doctor
de Launoy and Tillemont, to cast doubts on the
existence of Saint Catherine of Alexandria. For
my part, I am not inclined to go so far, and I hold
such an absolute denial as rash. I recognise that the

biography of this saint has come to us from the
East overlaid everywhere with fabulous details, but I
believe that these embellishments have been laid over
a solid foundation.   Neither Launoy nor Tillemont
is infallible.   It is not certain that Saint Catherine
never existed, and if by chance historic proof of her
non-existence were established, that would give way
before the theological testimony to the contrary,
furnished by the miraculous appearances of this
saint authenticated by the Ordinary and solemnly
recognised by the Pope.   For, after all, good logic
requires that truths of the scientific plane should
yield to truths of a higher order.   But we are not
yet in a position to know the opinion of the Church
as to the Maid's apparitions.   Jeanne d'Arc has not
been canonised, and the miracles wrought for her or
by her are open to discussion : I neither deny nor
affirm them, and it is a purely human vision which
makes me perceive in the history of this marvellous
girl the hand of God stretched out over France.
Truth to tell, though, that vision is powerful and
penetrating."

M. BERGERET: "If I have rightly understood you,
monsieur l'abbé, you do not consider the strange
event at Fierbois as an attested miracle, when Jeanne,
as they say, pointed out a sword concealed in the
wall.   And you are not certain that the Maid, as
she herself declared, brought back a child to life at

Lagny. You know my opinions, and for my part I should give a natural interpretation to these two facts. I suppose that the sword was fastened to the wall of the Church as a votive offering, and was consequently visible. As for the child that the Maid raised from the dead for the time necessary for the administration of baptism, and who died again after having been brought to the font, I confine myself to reminding you that there was near Domremy a Notre-Dame-des-Aviots whose particular function it was to endow still-born children with a few hours of life. I suspect that the memory of Notre-Dame-des-Aviots had a good deal to do with the illusions that possessed Jeanne d'Arc when she believed, at Lagny, that she had raised a new-born child from the dead."

M. LANTAIGNE : "There is much uncertainty in these explanations, monsieur. And rather than adopt them, I suspend my judgment, which inclines, I confess, towards the miraculous side, at least with respect to Saint Catherine's sword. For the passage is precise : the sword was *in* the wall, and it was necessary to excavate to find it. Neither is it impossible, again, that God, upon the efficacious prayers of a virgin, should have given life back to a child that had died without having received baptism."

M. BERGERET : "You speak, monsieur l'abbé, of

' the efficacious prayers of a virgin.' Do you then grant, in accordance with the belief of the Middle Ages, that there was some virtue, some peculiar power, in Jeanne d'Arc's virginity ? "

M. LANTAIGNE : "Clearly virginity is pleasing to God, and Jesus Christ rejoices in the triumph of His virgins. A young girl turned Attila and his Huns back from Lutetia ; a young girl delivered Orleans and caused the lawful king to be crowned at Rheims."

The priest having thus expressed himself, M. Bergeret seized on his words in a way of his own.

"Exactly," said he. " Jeanne d'Arc was a mascotte."

But Abbé Lantaigne did not hear. He rose and said :

"France's destined rôle in Christendom is not yet achieved. I foresee that ere long God will yet again work His will through the nation which has been the most faithful and the most faithless to Him."

"And so it is," answered M. Bergeret, "that, as in the profligate times of King Charles VII., we behold the rise of prophetesses. Our town indeed holds one of them, who is making a happier start than Jeanne, since Jacquot d'Arc's daughter was regarded as mad by her parents, and Mademoiselle Deniseau finds a disciple in her own father. Still I do not believe that her good luck will be great and lasting. Our *préfet*, M. Worms-Clavelin, is somewhat wanting in good breeding, but he is less of a simpleton than Baudricourt, and it is no longer the custom for the heads of the State to give audience to prophetesses. M. Félix Faure will not be advised by his confessor to test Mademoiselle Deniseau. Here, perhaps, you may reply, monsieur l'abbé, that the influence of Bernadette of Lourdes is stronger in our days than that of Jeanne d'Arc ever was. The latter overthrew some hundreds of starving and panic-stricken English; Bernadette has set countless pilgrims on the march and drawn thousands of millions to a mountain in the Pyrenees. And my revered friend, M. Pierre Laffitte, assures me that we have entered on an era of positive philosophy."

"As for what happens at Lourdes," said Abbé Lantaigne, "without becoming latitudinarian or falling into excessive credulity, I reserve my opinion on a point upon which the Church has made no pronouncement. But henceforth I see a triumph for religion in this crowd of pilgrims, just as you yourself see in it a defeat for materialistic philosophy."

XI

HE ministry had fallen. M. *le préfet* Worms-Clavelin felt neither surprise nor regret at this. In the depths of his heart he had always considered it too restless and too disturbing, an object of suspicion, and not without reason, to the agriculturist, the large merchant, and the small investor. Without affecting the fortunate indifference of the masses, this cabinet had exercised, to the *préfet's* grief, a vexatious influence over freemasonry, the organisation by which, for fifteen years past, the whole political life of the department had been drawn together and held in check. M. *le préfet* Worms-Clavelin had been able to turn the masonic lodges of the department into boards vested with the preliminary choice of candidates for public offices, for electoral functions, and for party favours. Exercising in this way wide and definite prerogatives, the lodges, being as much opportunist as they were radical, combined, acted in concert with one another, and worked together for the

republican cause. The *préfet*, rejoicing to see the ambition of some restraining the desires of others, gathered together, on the joint recommendation of the lodges, a band of senators, deputies, municipal councillors and road-surveyors, all equally loyal to the government, yet sufficiently diverse in opinion and sufficiently moderate to satisfy and reassure all republican parties, save the socialists. M. *le préfet* Worms-Clavelin had brought about this unanimity. And now the radical ministry must needs break up so happy a harmony.

Ill-luck decreed that the holder of one of the minor portfolios (either agriculture or commerce) should travel through the department and stop for some hours in the county town. It sufficed for him to deliver a philosophic and moral speech at one assembly to flutter all the assemblies, divide each lodge into two, set brother against brother, and infuriate citizen Mandar, the chemist of the Rue Culture, master of the lodge "New Alliance," and a radical, against M. Tricoul, vine-grower of Les Tournelles, master of the lodge "Sacred Friendship," and an opportunist.

Mentally M. Worms-Clavelin made another complaint against the fallen ministry : that of having lavishly distributed academic decorations and given Orders of Merit for agricultural proficiency to radical-socialists only, thus robbing the *préfet* of the advantage of governing with the aid of these decorations, or at least by means of tardily fulfilled promises of them.

M. *le préfet* expressed his thoughts accurately as, alone in his study, he murmured these bitter words :

"If they believed they could play at politics by upsetting my loyal lodges and fastening my useful palms to the tail of every drunken dog in the department, they'll find themselves finely mistaken ! "

Thus it was that he heard of the fall of the ministry without any regret.

Besides, these changes that he had foreseen never surprised him. His administrative policy was always founded on the assumption that minister succeeds minister. He made a point of never serving a Home Secretary with ardent zeal. He refrained from being over-pleasing to any one, and shunned all opportunities of doing too well. This moderation, kept up during the continuance of one ministry, assured him the sympathy of the next one, thus sufficiently predisposed in his favour to acquiesce in its turn in the half-hearted zeal, which became a claim to the favour of a third cabinet. M. *le préfet* Worms-Clavelin reigned without ruling, corresponded briefly with the Place Beauvau,* manœuvred the boards, and stayed in office.

In his study, through the half-open windows of which came the scent of flowering lilacs and the

* Where the French Home Office is situated.

twittering of sparrows, he was meditating, in a gentle and peaceful mood, on the lingering extinction of the scandals which on two occasions had gone near to ruining the leaders of the party. He looked forward to the day, still far distant, on which it would again be possible to resume activity. He reflected that, in spite of passing difficulties, and notwithstanding the discord unluckily communicated to the masonic lodges and the electoral committees, he would have capital municipal elections. The mayors in this agricultural district were excellent. The spirit of the populace was so loyal that the two deputies, who, being compromised in several financial transactions, were threatened with legal proceedings, had yet retained all their influence in their districts. He said to himself that the *scrutin de liste** would never have produced such favourable results. In his exaltation of mind thoughts that were almost philosophic came to the surface of his mind as to the ease with which men can be governed. He had a confused vision of this human beast allowing itself to be led, and straggling along in tireless gloomy tractableness beneath the eye of the shepherding dog.

M. Lacarelle entered the study with a newspaper in his hand.

" Monsieur *le préfet*, the resignation of the ministers,

---

* In which each voter inscribes on his paper as many names as there are vacancies to be filled.

having been accepted by the President of the Republic, is announced in *l'Officiel*."

M. *le préfet* Worms-Clavelin continued his gentle musing, and M. Lacarelle turned up his long Gallic moustaches and rolled his china-blue eyes, as a sign that he was about to give expression to a thought. And, as a matter of fact, he did so.

" Opinions differ as to the fall of the ministry."

"Really ? " asked M. *le préfet*, who was not listening.

"Well ! monsieur *le préfet*, it cannot be denied that Mademoiselle Claudine Deniseau predicted that the ministry would fall at an early date."

M. *le préfet* shrugged his shoulders. He had a mind wise enough to see that there was nothing marvellous in the fulfilment of such a prophecy. But Lacarelle, with a profound knowledge of local affairs, a marvellously contagious stupidity, and an exceptional aptitude for self-delusion, immediately related to him three or four new stories which were running through the town, and especially the story of M. de Gromance, to whom, Saint Radegonde had said, in reply to her visitor's secret thought : "Be at ease, monsieur *le comte ;* the child that your wife will bear is really your son." Then Lacarelle returned to the disclosure of the hidden treasure. Two Roman coins had been found at the place indicated. The excavations were still going on.

There had also been some cures of which the private secretary gave vague and rambling descriptions.

M. *le préfet* Worms-Clavelin listened uncomprehendingly. The mere idea of the Deniseau girl saddened and worried him. The influence of this visionary over the townsfolk at large was beyond his understanding. He was afraid of using his abilities ineffectively in a psychic case such as this. This fear paralysed his reason, although it was strong enough in ordinary circumstances. As he listened to Lacarelle, he experienced a dread of being convinced, and instinctively exclaimed brusquely :

" I don't believe in such things as these ! I don't believe in them ! "

But doubt and anxiety overwhelmed him. He wished to know what Abbé Guitrel, whom he regarded as both learned and intelligent, thought on the subject of this prophetess. It was just the time when he would meet the abbé at the goldsmith's house. He went to Rondonneau junior's, and found him in the inner room, nailing up a case, whilst Abbé Guitrel examined a silver-gilt vase set on a long stem and surmounted with a rounded lid.

"That's a fine chalice, isn't it, monsieur l'abbé ?"

" It is a pyx, monsieur *le préfet*, a ciborium, a vessel intended *ad ferendos cibos*.* In fact, the pyx holds the sacred hosts, the food of the soul.

* To bear the bread.

Formerly they used to keep the pyx in a silver dove hung over the baptismal font, the altar, or the tomb of a martyr. This one is decorated in the style of the thirteenth century. An austere and magnificent style, very suitable, monsieur *le préfet*, for church furniture, and especially for the sacred vessels."

M. Worms-Clavelin was not listening to the priest, whose restless, crafty profile he was observing. "Here is the man," thought he, "who is going to tell me about Saint Radegonde and the prophetess." And the departmental representative of the Republic was already screwing up his courage, concentrating his energies, lest he should appear weak-minded, superstitious and credulous, before an ecclesiastic.

"Yes, monsieur *le préfet*," said Abbé Guitrel, "our worthy M. Rondonneau junior has executed this beautiful specimen of goldsmith's work after ancient models. I am inclined to think that they could not have done better in the Place Saint-Sulpice, in Paris, where the best goldsmiths are to be found."

"*À propos*, monsieur l'abbé, what is your opinion of the prophetess whom our town possesses ?"

"What prophetess, monsieur *le préfet ?* Do you mean that poor girl who pretends to be in communication with Saint Radegonde, queen of France ? Alas ! monsieur, it cannot possibly be the pious spouse of Clotaire who suggests to that miserable girl sorry nonsense of every kind and rhapsodies which, being irreconcilable with good sense, are still less to be reconciled with theology. Foolery, monsieur *le préfet*, mere foolery ! "

M. Worms-Clavelin, who had prepared some subtle jests concerning priestly credulity, remained silent.

" No, indeed," continued M. Guitrel, with a smile, " it is incredible that Saint Radegonde should suggest this trash, this folly, all these silly, empty, sometimes heterodox, speeches that fall from the lips of this young maiden. The voice of the sainted Radegonde would have another accent, believe me."

M. LE PRÉFET : "Very little is known, in fact, about this Saint Radegonde."

M. GUITREL : "You mistake, monsieur *le préfet*, you mistake ! Saint Radegonde, reverenced by the whole Catholic Church, is the object of special worship in the diocese of Poitiers, which was formerly witness of her merits."

M. LE PRÉFET : "Yes, as you say, monsieur l'abbé, there is a special . . ."

M. GUITREL : "Even atheists themselves have regarded this great figure with admiration. What a sublime picture, monsieur *le préfet !* After the murder of her brother by her husband, Clotaire's noble spouse betakes herself to Bishop Médard at Noyon, and urges him to dedicate her to God. Taken by surprise, Saint Médard hesitates ; he

urges the indissolubility of marriage. But Radegonde herself covers her head with the veil of a
recluse, and flings herself at the feet of the pontiff,
who, overcome by the saintly persistence of the
queen, and braving the wrath of the savage monarch,
offers this blessed victim to God."

M. LE PRÉFET : "But, monsieur l'abbé, do you
approve of a bishop defying the civil powers in that
fashion and abetting the wife of his overlord in her
revolt ? The deuce ! if these are your opinions, I
shall be grateful to you for telling me so."

M. GUITREL : "Alas ! monsieur *le préfet*, I have
not, as the blessed Médard had, the illumination of
sanctity to enable me to discern the will of God in
extraordinary circumstances. Luckily nowadays the
rules which a bishop should follow with regard to
the civil powers are definitely defined. And monsieur *le préfet* will kindly remember, in speaking of
me for the bishopric of Tourcoing to his friends in
the ministry, that I recognise all the obligations that
follow from the Concordat. But why intrude my
humble personality in these great scenes of history ?
Saint Radegonde, clothed in the veil of a deaconess,
founded the monastery of Sainte-Croix in Poitiers,
where she lived for more than fifty years in the
practice of a rigorous asceticism. She observed
fasts and abstinences with such scrupulousness . . ."

M. LE PRÉFET : "Keep these stories of yours,

monsieur l'abbé, for your seminarists. You don't believe that Saint Radegonde communicates with Mademoiselle Deniseau. I congratulate you on that. And I could wish that all the priests in the department were as reasonable as you. But it only needs this hysteric patient—for hysteric she is—to attack the government for all the curés to come in herds to listen, open-mouthed and applauding, to all the insults she spits out."

M. GUITREL: "Oh! they make reservations, monsieur *le préfet*, they make reservations. The Church instructs them to be extremely wary in face of every fact that assumes the appearance of a miracle. And I assure you that, for my part, I am very distrustful of modern miracles."

M. LE PRÉFET: "Tell me, between ourselves: you don't believe in miracles, my dear abbé?"

M. GUITREL: "In miracles that are not duly verified I have, indeed, but little belief."

M. LE PRÉFET: "We are alone. Confess, now, that there are no miracles, that there never have been any, and that there never can possibly be any."

M. GUITREL: "Not at all, monsieur *le préfet*. A miracle is possible; it can be unmistakably recognised; it is useful for the confirmation of doctrine; and its utility is proved by the conversion of nations."

M. LE PRÉFET: "Anyhow, you grant that it is

ridiculous to believe that Saint Radegonde, who lived in the Middle Ages . . ."

M. GUITREL : " In the sixth century, in the sixth century."

M. LE PRÉFET : " Exactly, in the sixth century. . . . should come in 189– to gossip with the daughter of a registry-keeper on the political programme of the ministry and the Chambers."

M. GUITREL : "Communications between the Church triumphant and the Church militant are possible ; history supplies numberless undeniable instances of it.   But, yet again, I do not believe that the young person of whom we are speaking is favoured with a communication of this kind.   Her sayings, if I may dare to say so, do not bear the hall-mark of a celestial revelation.   Everything she says is some-how . . ."

M. LE. PRÉFET : " Humbug."

M. GUITREL : " If you like. . . . Though, indeed, it might be quite possible that she is possessed."

M. LE PRÉFET : " What is this that you are saying ? You, an intelligent priest, a future bishop of the Republic, you believe in possession ! It is a mediæval superstition ! I have read a book by Michelet on it."

M. GUITREL : " But, monsieur *le préfet*, possession is a fact recognised not only by theologians, but also by scientists, atheists for the most part. And Michelet himself, whom you quote, believed in the cases of possession at Loudun."

M. LE PRÉFET : "What notions ! You are all the same ! And if Claudine Deniseau were possessed, as you say ? . . ."

M. GUITREL : "Then it would be necessary to exorcise her."

M. LE PRÉFET : "Exorcise her ? Don't you think, monsieur l'abbé, that that would be absurd ? "

M. GUITREL : "Not at all, monsieur *le préfet*, not at all."

M. LE PRÉFET : "What does one do ? "

M. GUITREL : "There are rules, monsieur *le préfet*, a formulary, a ritual for this kind of operation, which has never ceased to be used. Jeanne d'Arc herself had to undergo it, in the town of Vaucouleurs, unless I mistake. M. Laprune, the curé of Saint-Exupère, would be the right person to exorcise this Deniseau girl, who is one of his parishioners. He is a very venerable priest. It is true that, as regards the Deniseau family, he is in a position which may react on his character, and, to a certain extent, influence a wise and cautious mind, as yet unenfeebled by age, or which at any rate still seems able to bear the weight of years and the fatigues of a long and onerous ministry. I mean to say that events, regarded by some as miracles, have taken place in the parish of this worthy curé ; and M. Laprune's zeal must needs have been

led into error by the thought that the parish of
Saint-Exupère may have been privileged to such a
degree that a manifestation of divine power has
taken place in it, in preference to all the other parishes
in our town. Buoyed up by such a hope, he has
perhaps formed illusions which he has unconsciously
communicated to his clergy. An error and a mistake
which one can excuse, if one considers the circumstances. Indeed, what blessings would not a new
miracle shed on the parish church of Saint-Exupère !
The zeal of the faithful would be revived by it, an
outpouring of gifts would bring wealth into the
famous, but clean-stripped, walls of the ancient
church. And the favour of the Cardinal-Archbishop
would solace the last days of M. Laprune, now arrived
at the end of his ministry and strength."

M. LE PRÉFET : " But if I understand you rightly,
monsieur l'abbé, it is this doddering curé of Saint-
Exupère, it is M. Laprune, with his vicaires, who has
got up the affair of the Prophetess. Undoubtedly
the priests are strong. They won't believe it in
Paris, in the bureaux, but it is the truth. The priests
are a fine power ! Here your old Laprune has been
organising these séances of clerical spiritualism which
all the town attends in order to hear the Parliament,
the presidency, and myself insulted—for I am perfectly
aware that they don't spare me in these conventicles
of the Place Saint-Exupère."

M. GUITREL : "Oh! monsieur *le préfet*, far be it from me to think of suspecting the worthy curé of Saint-Exupère of having concocted a plot! On the contrary, I sincerely believe that, if he has in any way encouraged this unhappy affair, he will soon recognise his error, and will use all his influence to efface the results of it. . . . But even in his interest and in that of the diocese, one might forestall him and inform His Eminence of the real facts, of which he is perhaps still ignorant. Once warned of these disorders, he will doubtless put an end to them."

M. LE PRÉFET : "That's an idea! . . . My dear abbé, are you willing to undertake the commission? For my part, as *préfet*, I am obliged to ignore the fact that there is an Archbishop, save in cases provided for by the law, such as bells and processions. When one thinks of it, it is an absurd situation, for from the moment that Archbishops have an actual existence . . . But politics have their necessities. Tell me frankly. Are you in favour at the Archbishop's palace?"

M. GUITREL : "His Eminence sometimes deigns to listen to me with kindness. The affability of His Eminence is extreme."

M. LE PRÉFET : "Well! tell him that it is inadmissible for Saint Radegonde to come to life again in order to plague the senators, the deputies, and the *préfet* of the department, and that, in the interests of the Church as well as of the Republic, it is time to bridle the tongue of the fierce Clotaire's spouse. Just tell His Eminence that."

M. GUITREL. "Substantially, monsieur *le préfet;* substantially I will tell him that."

M. LE PRÉFET : " Set about it as you like, monsieur l'abbé, but prove to him that he must forbid his priests to enter the Deniseau house, that he must openly reprimand the curé Laprune, condemn in *la Semaine religieuse* the speeches made by this mad woman, and officially request the editors of *le Libéral* to cease the campaign they are waging in support of a miracle both unconstitutional and contrary to the Concordat."

M. GUITREL : " I will try it, monsieur *le préfet.* Certainly, I will try it. But what am I, a poor professor of sacred rhetoric, before His Eminence the Cardinal-Archbishop ?"

M. LE PRÉFET : " He is intelligent, is your Archbishop ; he will understand that his own interests, and the honour of Saint Radegonde, by the Lord ! . . ."

M. GUITREL : "Doubtless, monsieur *le préfet,* doubtless. But His Eminence, so devoted to the spiritual interests of the diocese, perhaps considers that the prodigious crowd of souls around this poor girl is a token of that yearning after belief which torments the younger generation, a proof that faith is more living than ever among the masses, an example, in fact, which it would be well to present to the consideration of statesmen. And it is possible that, thinking thus, he may be in no hurry to cause the sign to cease, to suppress the proof and the example. It is possible . . ."

M. LE PRÉFET : " . . . that he may make fun of everybody. He is quite capable of it."

M. GUITREL : "Oh ! monsieur *le préfet*, there is no foundation for that assumption ! But how much easier and more certain would my mission be, if, like the dove from the ark, I were the bearer of an olive branch, if I were authorised to say—oh ! just in a whisper !—to Monseigneur, that the salary of the seven poor curés of the diocese, suspended by the former Minister of Religion, was restored ! "

M. LE PRÉFET : " Give, give, that's it, isn't it ? I will think it over. . . . I will telegraph to Paris, and I will bring you the answer at Rondonneau junior's. Good evening, monsieur *le diplomate !* "

A week after the day of this secret conference Abbé Guitrel had successfully accomplished his mission. The prophetess of the Place Saint-Exupère, disowned by the archbishopric, abandoned by the clergy, abjured by *le Libéral*, kept on her side none save the two corresponding members of the academy of psychical research, one of whom regarded her as a subject worthy of study and the

I

other as a dangerous charlatan. Freed from this
mad woman, and delighted at the municipal elections,
which had brought forth neither new measures nor
new men, M. *le préfet* Worms-Clavelin rejoiced from
the bottom of his heart.

XII

PAILLOT was the bookseller at the corner of the Place Saint-Exupère and the Rue des Tintelleries. For the most part the houses which surrounded this square were ancient; those that leant against the church bore carved and painted signboards. Several had a pointed gable and a wooden frontage. One of these, which had kept its carved beams, was a gem admired by connoisseurs. The main joists were upheld by carved corbels, some in the shape of angels bearing shields, the others in the form of monks crouching low. To the left of the door, against a post, rose the mutilated figure of a woman, her brow encircled by a floreated crown. The townsfolk declared that this was Queen Marguerite. And the building was known by the name of Queen Marguerite's house.

It was believed, on the authority of Dom Maurice, author of a *Trésor d'antiquités*, printed in 1703, that Margaret of Scotland lodged in this house for several months of the year 1438. But M. de

Terremondre, president of the Society of Agriculture and Archæology, proves in a substantially constructed memoir that this house was built in 1488 for a prominent citizen named Philippe Tricouillard. The archæologists of the town, whenever they conduct sightseers to the front of this building, seizing a moment when the ladies are inattentive, take pleasure in showing the canting arms of Philippe Tricouillard, carved on a shield held by two angels. These arms, which M. de Terremondre has judiciously compared with those of the Coleoni of Bergamo, are represented on the corbel which stands over the doorway, under the left lintel. The figures on it are very shadowy, and are only recognisable by those who have had them pointed out. As for the figure of a woman wearing a crown, which leans against the perpendicular joist, M. de Terremondre found no difficulty in proving that it must be regarded as a Saint Marguerite. In fact, there may still be made out at the feet of the saint the remains of a hideous shape which is none other than that of the devil ; and the right arm of the principal figure, which is lacking to-day, ought to hold the holy-water sprinkler which the blessed saint shook over the enemy of the human race. It is clear what Saint Marguerite typifies in this place, now that M. Mazure, the archivist of the department, has brought to light a document proving that in the year 1488

Philippe Tricouillard, then about seventy years of age, had lately married Marguerite Larrivée, daughter of a magistrate.   By a confusion which is not very surprising, Marguerite Larrivée's celestial patron was taken for the young princess of Scotland whose sojourn in the town of . . . has left a deep impression.   Few ladies have bequeathed a memory more full of pity than that princess who died at twenty with this last sigh on her lips : " Out upon thee, life ! "

The house of M. Paillot, the bookseller, joins on to Queen Marguerite's house.   Originally it was built, like its neighbour, with a wooden front, and the visible timber-work was no less carefully carved. But, in 1860, M. Paillot's father, bookseller to the Archbishopric, had it pulled down in order to rebuild it simply, in the modern style, without any pretence at wealth or art, merely taking care to make it convenient as a dwelling-house and place of business. A tree of Jesse, in Renaissance style, which covered the entire front of Paillot's house, at the corner formed by the Place Saint-Exupère and the Rue des Tintelleries, was torn down with the rest, but not destroyed.   M. de Terremondre, coming upon it afterwards in a timber-merchant's yard, purchased it for the museum.   This monument is in good style. Unfortunately the prophets and patriarchs, who cluster on each branch like marvellous fruits, and

the Virgin, blossoming on the summit of the pro-
phetic tree, were mutilated by the Terrorists in
1793, and the tree suffered fresh damage in 1860,
when it was carried to the timber-yard as firewood.
M. Quatrebarbe, the diocesan architect, expatiates on
these mutilations in his interesting pamphlet on *Les
Vandales modernes*. "One shudders," says he, "at
the thought that this precious relic of an age of
faith ran the risk of being sawn up and burnt before
our very eyes."

This sentiment, being expressed by a man whose
clerical tendencies were well known, was trenchantly
criticised by *le Phare* in an anonymous paragraph in
which was recognised, rightly or wrongly, the hand
of the archivist of the department, M. Mazure.
"In twenty words," said this paragraph, "the
architect of the diocese supplies us with several
occasions for surprise. The first is that any one
should be able to shudder at the mere idea of the
loss of an indifferently carved beam, and one so
much mutilated that the details are not recognisable ;
the second is that this beam should stand to M.
Quatrebarbe, whose creed is well known, as a relic
of an age of faith, since it dates from 1530—that
is to say, from the year when the Protestant Diet
of Augsburg assembled ; the third is that M.
Quatrebarbe should omit to say that the precious
beam was torn down and sent to the timber-yard

by his own father-in-law, M. Nicolet, the diocesan architect, who, in 1860, transformed the Paillot house in the way which one can now see ; the fourth is that M. Quatrebarbe ignores the fact that it was none other than M. Mazure, the archivist, who discovered the carved beam in Clouzot's wood-yard, where it had been rotting for ten years under M. Quatrebarbe's very nose, and who pointed it out to M. de Terremondre, president of the Society of Agriculture and Archæology, who purchased it for the museum."

In its actual condition the house of M. Paillot, the bookseller, showed a uniform white frontage, three storeys in height. The shop, ornamented with wood-work painted green, bore, in letters of gold, the words, " Paillot, libraire."   The shop-window displayed ter-restrial and celestial globes of different diameters, boxes of mathematical instruments, school books and little text-books for the officers of the garrison, with a few novels and new memoirs : these were what M. Paillot called works of literature. A window, narrower and not so deep, that gave on the Rue des Tintelleries, contained works on agriculture and law, and thus completed the supply of instruments required by the intellectual life of the county town. On a counter inside the shop were to be found works of literature, novels, essays, and memoirs.

" Classics in sets " were stacked in pigeon-holes, and

quite at the bottom, by the side of the door which
opened on the staircase, some shelves were reserved
for old books.   For M. Paillot combined in his shop
the business of a new and second-hand bookseller.
This dark corner of the old books attracted the
bibliophiles of the district, who in days gone by had
found treasure-trove there.   A certain copy of the
first edition of the third book of Pantagruel was
recalled, unearthed in excellent condition in 1871 by
M. de Terremondre, father of the present president
of the Agricultural Society, at Paillot's, in the old-
book corner.   There was still more mysterious talk of
a Mellin de Saint-Gelais, containing on the back of
the title-page some autograph verses by Marie Stuart,
that M. Dutilleul, the notary, had found, about the
same time, and in the same place, and for which he
paid three francs.   But, since then, no one had
announced any marvellous discovery.   The gloomy,
monotonous corner of the old books scarcely changed.
There was always to be seen there *l'Abrégé de
l'Histoire des Voyages*, in fifty-six volumes, and the odd
volumes of Kehl's Voltaire, in large paper.   M.
Dutilleul's discovery, doubted by many, was by some
openly denied.   They based their opinion on the idea
that the old notary was quite capable of having lied
through vanity, and on the fact that after M. Dutilleul's
death no copy of the poems of Mellin de Saint-
Gelais was found in his library.   Yet the bibliophiles

of the town, who frequented Paillot's shop, never
failed to explore the old-book corner, at least once a
month.   M. de Terremondre was one of the most
assiduous visitors.

He was a large landed proprietor in the department, well connected, a breeder of cattle and a
connoisseur in artistic matters.   He it was who
designed the historic costumes for processions and
who presided over the committee formed for the
erection of a statue of Jeanne d'Arc on the ramparts.
He spent four months of the year in Paris, and had
the reputation of being a man of gallantry.   At fifty
he preserved a slim and elegant figure.   He was very
popular with all three classes in the county town,
and they had several times offered him the position
of deputy.   This he had refused, declaring that his
leisure, as well as his independence, was dear to him.
And people were curious about the reasons for his
refusal.

M. de Terremondre had thought of buying Queen
Marguerite's house in order to turn it into a museum
of local archæology and offer it to the town.   But
Madame Houssieu, the widowed owner of this house,
had not responded to the overtures which he had made
to her.   Now more than eighty years of age, she lived
in the old house, alone, save for a dozen cats.   She
was supposed to be rich and miserly.   All that could
be done was to wait for her death.   Every time that

he entered Paillot's shop, M. de Terremondre asked the bookseller :

" Is Queen Marguerite still in the land of the living ? "

And M. Paillot replied that assuredly one morning she would be found dead in her bed, living shut up alone at her age.   Meanwhile, he dreaded her setting his house on fire.   This was her neighbour's constant fear.   He lived in terror lest the old lady should burn down her wooden house and his along with it.

Madame Houssieu interested M. de Terremondre greatly.   He was inquisitive about all that Queen Marguerite, as he called her, said and did.   At the last visit which he had paid to her, she had shown him a bad Restoration engraving representing the Duchess of Angoulême pressing to her heart the portraits of Louis XVI. and Marie Antoinette enclosed in a medallion.   This engraving, set in a black frame, hung in the ground-floor sitting-room. Showing it to him, Madame Houssieu said :

" That's the portrait of Queen Marguerite, who long ago lived in this house."

And M. de Terremondre asked himself how a portrait of Marie-Thérèse-Charlotte of France had, even by the dullest of minds, been taken for a portrait of Margaret of Scotland.   He meditated on it for a month.

Then one day he exclaimed, as he entered Paillot's shop :

" I've got it ! "

And he explained to his friend the bookseller the very plausible reasons for this extraordinary confusion.

" Listen to me, Paillot ! Margaret of Scotland, mistaken for Marguerite Larrivée, is confused with Marguerite of Valois, Duchess of Angoulême, and this princess is, in her turn, confused with the Duchess of Angoulême, daughter of Louis XVI. and Marie-Antoinette, Marguerite Larrivée—Margaret of Scotland—Marguerite, Duchess of Angoulême— the Duchess of Angoulême.

" I am rather proud of having found that out, Paillot. Tradition should always be taken into account. But when we own Queen Marguerite's house, we will furbish up the memory of that good Philippe Tricouillard a little."

Hard upon this declaration Dr. Fornerol entered the shop with the wonted impetuosity of that indefatigable visitor of the sick, who brought with him hope and comfort. Gustave Fornerol was a fat, moustachioed man. Possessed in his wife's right of a small country estate, he affected the fashions of a country proprietor and paid his visits in a soft hat, a hunting waistcoat and leather leggings. Although his practice was exclusively among the lower middle class and the rural population of the suburbs, he was considered the most skilful practitioner in the town.

Friendly with Paillot, as with all his fellow-townsmen, he was not in the habit of paying useless visits to him, nor of wasting his time gossiping in the shop. This time, however, he sank down on one of the three rush-bottomed chairs which, set in the old-book corner, had gained for Paillot's shop the reputation for a hospitality at once literary, learned, cultured, and academic.

He puffed, waved a good-day to Paillot with his hand, bowed with some deference to M. de Terremondre, and said :

" I am tired. . . . Well ! Paillot, were you pleased with the show yesterday ? What did Madame Paillot think of the play and the actors ? "

The bookseller did not commit himself. He considered that it is wise for a tradesman to express no opinions in his shop. Besides, he went to the theatre only *en famille*, and that but seldom. But Dr. Fornerol, whose position as medical officer to the theatre procured him free passes, never missed a performance.

A travelling company had given *la Maréchale* the night before, with Pauline Giry in the leading part.

" She is always capital, is Pauline Giry," said the doctor.

"That's the general opinion," said the bookseller.

"She isn't as young as she once was," said M. de Terremondre, who was turning over the leaves of volume xxxviii. of *l'Histoire Générale des Voyages*.

"By Jove, no!" answered the doctor. "You know that Giry isn't her real name?"

"Her real name is Girou," answered M. de Terremondre authoritatively. "I knew her mother, Clémence Girou. Fifteen years ago Pauline Giry was dark and very pretty."

And the three of them, in the old-book corner, set to work to reckon the actress's age. But as they were calculating from doubtful or incorrect data, they only reached contradictory, or sometimes even absurd, conclusions, and with these they were by no means satisfied.

"I am worn out," said the doctor. "You all went to bed after the theatre. But I was called up at midnight to go to an old farmer on Duroc hill, who was suffering from strangulated hernia. Says his man to me: 'He has brought up everything he can. He harps on one note. He is going to die.' I have the horse put in and I spin out to Duroc hill, over yonder, right at the end of the Faubourg de Tramayes. I find my man a-bed and howling. Corpse-like face, stercoraceous vomiting. Very good! His wife says to me: 'It's in his inside that it takes him.'"

"She's forty-seven, is Pauline Giry," said M. de Terremondre.

"It's quite possible," said Paillot.

"At least forty-seven," answered the doctor. "Double hernia, and dangerous it was. Very good! I proceed to reduce it by hand-pressure. Although it is only necessary to exercise a very faint pressure with the hand, after thirty minutes of this business, one's arms and back are broken. And it was only at the end of five hours, at the tenth repetition, that I was able to effect the reduction."

At this point in the narrative recounted by Dr. Fornerol, Paillot the bookseller went to serve some ladies who asked for some interesting books to read in the country. And the doctor, addressing himself to M. de Terremondre alone, continued :

"I was one ache. I say to my man : 'You must keep to your bed, and, if possible, you must remain lying on your back, until the truss-maker has made a truss for you according to my directions. Lie stretched out, or look out for strangulation. And you know whether that's nice ! Without counting that one day or another it'll carry you off. You understand ?'

"'Yes, sir.'

"'Very good.'

"Down I go to the yard to wash myself at the pump. You may imagine that after this business I wanted a bit of a wash.   I strip myself to the waist, and I rub myself with soft soap for, maybe, a quarter of an hour.   I dress myself again.   I drink a glass of white wine that they bring me in the yard. I see the grey dawn break, I hear the lark sing, and I go back to the sick man's room.   There it was dark.   I shout in the direction of the bed : 'Hey ? That's understood, isn't it ?   Perfect stillness whilst waiting for the new truss.   The one you have is no good at all.   D'you hear ?'   No answer.   'Are you asleep ?'   Then I hear behind me the voice of the old nurse : 'Doctor, our man's no longer in the house,' she tells me.   'He was wearying to go out to his vines.'"

"There I recognise my peasants," said M. de Terremondre.

He lapsed into meditation and resumed :

"Doctor, Pauline Giry is now forty-nine.   She made her *début* at the Vaudeville in 1876 ; she was then twenty-two.   I am sure of it."

"In that case," said the doctor, "she would be in her forty-third year, since we are now in 1897."

"It isn't possible," said M. de Terremondre, "for she is at least six years older than Rose Max, who has certainly passed her fortieth year."

"Rose Max ?   I don't say no, but she is still a fine woman," said the doctor.

He yawned, stretched himself, and said :

"Getting back from Duroc hill, at six o'clock in the morning, I find two baker's men in my hall, come to tell me that their mistress, the baker's wife of the Tintelleries, has been brought to bed."

"But," asked M. de Terremondre, "did it require two baker's men to tell you that?"

"They had sent them one after the other," answered the doctor. "I ask if the characteristic symptoms have set in. They give me no answer, but a third baker's man turns up in his master's cart. Up I get and seat myself at his side. We take half a turn, and there I am rolling over the pavement of the Tintelleries."

"I have it!" exclaimed M. de Terremondre, who was pursuing his own thoughts. "It was in '69 that she came out at the Vaudeville. And it was in '76 that my cousin Courtrai knew her . . . and was intimate with her."

"Are you speaking of Jacques de Courtrai, who was a captain of dragoons?"

"No, I am speaking of Agénor, who died in Brazil. . . . She has a son who left Saint-Cyr last year."

Thus spoke M. de Terremondre, just as M. Bergeret, professor of literature at the University, entered the shop.

M. Bergeret held one of the three academic chairs of the Paillot establishment, and was the most indefatigable talker of the old-book corner.   There, with a friendly hand, he used to turn over the leaves of books old and books new, and although he never bought a single volume, for fear of getting a wigging for it from his wife and three daughters, he received the heartiest welcome from Paillot, who held him in high esteem as a reservoir, an alembic, of that science and those belles-lettres on which booksellers live and flourish.   The old-book corner was the only place in the town where M. Bergeret could sit in utter contentment, for at home Madame Bergeret chased him from room to room for different reasons of domestic administration; at the University, the Dean, in his hatred, forced him to give his lectures in a dark, unhealthy cellar, into which but few pupils descended, and all three classes in the town cast black looks at him for having called Jeanne d'Arc a military mascotte.   Now M. Bergeret slipped into the old-book corner.

"Good-day, gentlemen !   Anything new ?"

"A baby to the baker's wife in the Tintelleries," said the doctor.   "I brought it into the world just twenty minutes ago.   I was going to tell M. de Terremondre about it.   And I may add that it wasn't without difficulty."

"This child," replied the professor, "hesitated to be born.   He would never have consented to it if, being gifted with understanding and foresight, he

K

had known the destiny of man on the earth, and more especially in our town."

"It is a pretty little girl," said the doctor, "a pretty little girl with a raspberry mark under the left breast."

The conversation continued between the doctor and M. de Terremondre.

"A pretty little girl, with a raspberry mark under the left breast, doctor? It would seem that the bakeress had a longing for raspberries when she took off her corsets. The mere desire of a mother does not suffice to stamp the picture of it on the offspring she bears. It is also necessary that the longing woman should touch one particular part of her body. And the picture will be stamped on the child in the corresponding spot. Isn't that the common belief, doctor?"

"That is what old women believe," replied Dr. Fornerol. "And I have known men, and even doctors, who were women in this respect, and who shared in the credulity of the nurses. For my part, the experience of an already long practice, my knowledge of observations made by scientists, and especially a general view of embryology, prevent my sharing in this popular belief."

"Then, according to your opinion, doctor, wishing-marks are just spots like others, that form on the skin without known cause."

"Stop a bit !   'Wishing-marks' present a particular characteristic.   They contain no blood-vessels
and are not erectile, like the tumours with which
you might perhaps be tempted to confuse them."

"You declare, doctor, that they are a peculiar
species.   Do you make no inference from that as to
their origin ? "

"Absolutely none."

"But if these spots are not really 'wishing-marks,'
if you refuse them a . . . how shall I put it ? . . . a
psychic origin, I am unable to account for the accident
of a belief which is found in the Bible, and which is
still shared by such a great number of people.   My
aunt Pastré was a very intelligent and by no means
superstitious woman.   She died last spring, aged
seventy-seven, in the full belief that the three white
currants visible on the shoulder of her daughter
Bertha had an illustrious origin and came from the
Parc de Neuilly, where, in the autumn of 1834,
during her pregnancy, she was presented to Queen
Marie-Amélie, who took her to walk along a path
bordered by currant-bushes."

To this Dr. Fornerol made no reply.   He was
not remarkably given to contradicting the opinions
of rich patients.   But M. Bergeret, professor of
literature at the University, bent his head towards
his left shoulder and gave a far-away look, as he
always did whenever he was going to speak.   Then
he said :

" Gentlemen, it is a fact that these marks, called 'wishing-spots,' reduce themselves to a small number of types, which may be classified, according to their colour and form, into strawberries, currants, and raspberries, or wine and coffee spots. It would, perhaps, be convenient to add to these types that of those diffused yellow spots in which folks endeavour to recognise portions of tart or mince-pie. Now, who can possibly believe that pregnant women desire nothing save to drink wine or *café au lait*, or to eat red fruits, and, possibly, forcemeat-pie ? Such an idea runs counter to natural philosophy. That desire which, according to certain philosophers, has alone created the world and alone preserves it, works in them as in all living beings, only with more range and diversity. It gives them secret fevers, hidden passions, and strange frenzies. Without going into the question of the effect of their particular condition on the appetites common to all that lives, and even to plants, we recognise that this condition does not produce indifference, but that it rather perverts and inflames the deeper instincts. If the new-born child ought really to carry the visible signs of its mother's desires, believe me, we should more frequently see imprinted on its body other symbols than these innocent strawberries and drops of coffee with which the folly of old wives diverts itself."

"I see what you mean," said M. de Terremondre. "Women loving jewels, many children would be born with sapphires, rubies, and emeralds on their fingers, and with gold bracelets on their wrists ; necklaces of pearls, rivières of diamonds would cover their neck and breast. Still, one ought to be able to point to such children as these."

"Just so," replied M. Bergeret.

And, taking up from the table, where M. de Terremondre had left it, the thirty-eighth volume of *l'Histoire Générale des Voyages,* the professor buried his nose in the book, between pages 212 and 213, a spot which, every time that he had opened the inevitable old book during the last six years, had confronted him like a fate, to the exclusion of every other page, as an instance of the monotony with which life glides by, a symbol of the uniformity of those tasks and those days in a provincial university which precede the day of death and the travail of the body in the tomb. And this time, as he had already done so many times before, M. Bergeret read in volume xxxviii. of *l'Histoire Générale des Voyages* the first lines of page 212 : "a passage to the North. 'It is to this check,' said he, 'that we owe the opportunity of being able to visit the Sandwich Isles again, and to enrich our voyage with a discovery which, although the last, seems in many respects to be the most important that Europeans have yet made in the whole expanse of the Pacific Ocean.' The happy prophecy which these words seemed to denote has, unfortunately, never been fulfilled."

And this time, as always, the reading of these lines plunged M. Bergeret into melancholy. Whilst he was immersed in it, the bookseller, M. Paillot, confronted a little soldier, who had come in to buy a sou's worth of letter-paper, with disdain and hauteur.

"I don't keep letter-paper," declared M. Paillot, turning his back on the little soldier.

Then he complained of his assistant, Léon, who was always on errands, and who, once gone out, never came back. Consequently he, Paillot, was constantly being pestered by intruders. They actually asked him for letter-paper!

"I remember," said Dr. Fornerol to him, " that one market-day a good country-woman came in and asked you for a plaster, and that you had the greatest difficulty in preventing her from tucking up her petticoats and showing you the painful spot where the paper was to be applied."

Paillot, the bookseller, replied to this anecdotic sally by a silence which expressed offended dignity.

"Heavens!" exclaimed M. de Terremondre, the book-lover, "this learned storehouse of our Fröben, our Elzevir, our Debure, confused with the chemist's shop of Thomas Diafoirus! What an outrage!"

"Indeed," replied Dr. Fornerol, "the good soul meant no harm in showing Paillot the seat of her trouble. But it won't do to judge the peasants by her. In general, they show extreme repugnance to letting themselves be seen by the doctor. My country colleagues have often remarked this to me. Country-women, attacked by serious diseases, resist examination with an energy and obstinacy which townswomen, and particularly women of the world, do not show in the same circumstances. I saw a farmer's wife at Lucigny die of an internal tumour, which she had never allowed to be suspected."

M. de Terremondre, who, as president of several local academies, had literary prejudices, took these remarks as a pretext for accusing Zola of having shamefully maligned the peasants in *La Terre*. At this accusation, M. Bergeret emerged from his pensive sadness and said:

"Yet the peasants are drunkards and parricides, and voluntarily incestuous, as Zola has depicted them. Their repugnance to lend themselves to clinical inspection by no means proves their chastity. It only shows the power of prejudice in minds of limited intelligence. The simpler a prejudice is, the stronger is its power. The prejudice that it is wrong to be seen naked remains powerful with them. It has been weakened amongst artists and people of intelligence by the custom of baths, douches, and massage ; it has been still further weakened by æsthetic feeling and by the taste for voluptuous sensations, and it easily yields to considerations of health and hygiene. This is all that can be deduced from the doctor's observations."

"I have noticed," said M. de Terremondre, "that well-made women . . ."

"There are hardly any," said the doctor.

"Doctor, you remind me of my chiropodist," replied M. de Terremondre. "He said to me one day : 'If you were a chiropodist, sir, you would take no stock in women.'"

Paillot, the bookseller, who for some moments had been glued to the wall listening intently, said :

"I don't know what is going on in Queen Marguerite's house ; I hear cries and the noise of furniture being overturned."

And he was again seized with his customary misgiving.

"That old lady will set fire to her house, and the whole block of buildings will be burnt : it's all wood."

Nobody heeded these words, nobody attempted to soothe his ridiculous apprehensions. Dr. Fornerol rose painfully to his feet, stretched the wearied muscles of his arms with an effort, and went off on his round of visits through the town.

M. de Terremondre put on his gloves and took a step towards the door. Then, perceiving a tall withered figure which was crossing the square in stiff, abrupt strides :

"Here," said he, "is General Cartier de Chalmot. I hope the *préfet* won't meet him."

"And why not ?" demanded M. Bergeret.

"Because these meetings are by no means pleasant for M. Worms-Clavelin. Last Sunday our *préfet*, while driving by in a victoria, caught sight of General Cartier de Chalmot, who was walking with his wife and daughters. Lolling back in his carriage, with his hat on his head, he saluted the gallant veteran with a little wave of his hand and a ' Good-day, good-day, general !' The general reddened with anger. For the unassuming are always violent in their anger. General Chalmot was beside himself. He was terrible. Before all the promenaders he imitated M. Worms-Clavelin's familiar salute and shouted at him in a voice of thunder : ' Good-day, good-day, *préfet !* ' "

"There is perfect silence now in Queen Marguerite's house," said M. Paillot.

XIII

THE midday sun darted its clear white rays. Not a cloud in the sky, not a breath in the air. The solitary orb swung across the vast repose in which everything was wrapped and urged its blazing course towards the horizon. On the deserted Mall the shadows lay still and heavy at the foot of the elms. A road-mender slept in the bottom of the ditch that bounds the ramparts. The birds were silent.

Seated at the shady end of a bench three parts steeped in sunlight, M. Bergeret forgot, under these classic trees, in the friendly solitude, his wife and his three daughters, his cramped life and his cramped home; like Æsop he revelled in the freedom of his mind, and his analytical imagination roved irresponsibly among the living and the dead.

However Abbé Lantaigne, head of the high seminary, was passing, with his breviary in his hand, down the broad walk of the Mall. M. Bergeret rose to offer his shady place on the bench to the priest. M. Lantaigne came up and sank into it composedly, with that priestly dignity which never left him and which in him was just simplicity. M. Bergeret sat near him, at the spot where the shadow fell mingled with light from the feathery end of the branches, so that his black clothing was covered with golden discs, and over his dazzled eyes his eyelids began to blink.

He congratulated Abbé Lantaigne in these words :

"It is said everywhere, monsieur l'abbé, that you will be called to the bishopric of Tourcoing.

"The sign I hail, and from it dare to hope.*

But this choice is too good a one not to make one doubtful. You are believed to be a royalist, and that counts against you. Are you not a republican like the Pope?"

M. LANTAIGNE : "I am a republican like the Pope. That is to say, I am at peace and not at war with the government of the Republic. But peace is not love. And I do not love the Republic."

M. BERGERET : "I guess your reasons. You condemn it for being freethinking and hostile to the clergy."

M. LANTAIGNE : "Assuredly I condemn it as irreligious and inimical to the priests. But this irreligion, these hostilities, are not inherent in it.

* "J'en accepte l'augure et j'ose l'espérer."

They are the attributes of republicans, not of the Republic. They diminish or increase at every change of ministers. They are less to-day than they were yesterday. Possibly they will increase to-morrow. Perhaps a time will come when they will be non-existent, as they were non-existent under the rule of Marshal MacMahon, or at least during the delusive beginnings of that rule and under the deceptive ministry of May 16th. They are accidental, not essential. But even if it were respectful towards religion and its ministers, I should still hate the Republic."

M. BERGERET : "Why?"

M. LANTAIGNE : "Because it is diversity. In that it is essentially bad."

M. BERGERET : "I don't quite understand you, monsieur l'abbé."

M. LANTAIGNE : "That comes from your not having the theological mind. At one time even laymen received some impress of it. Their college note-books, which they preserved, supplied them with the elements of philosophy. That is especially true of the men of the seventeenth century. At that time all those who were educated knew how to reason, even the poets. It is the teaching of Port-Royal that underlies the *Phèdre* of Racine. But to-day when theology has been relegated to the seminaries, no one knows how to reason, and men of

THE ELM-TREE ON THE MALL   151

the world are almost as foolish as poets and savants. Did not M. de Terremondre, believing that he was speaking to the point, tell me yesterday, on the Mall, that Church and State ought to make mutual concessions ? People no longer know, they no longer think. Empty words pass and repass in the air. We are in Babel. You, Monsieur Bergeret, are much better read in Voltaire than in Saint Thomas."

M. BERGERET : "It is true.   But did you not say, monsieur l'abbé, that the Republic is *diversity*, and that in that respect it is essentially bad ?   That is what I beg you to explain to me.   Perhaps I might succeed in understanding you.   I know more theology than you credit me with.   Note-book in hand, I have read Baronius."

M. LANTAIGNE : "Baronius is only an annalist, although the greatest of all ; and I am quite sure that from him you have only been able to carry away some historic odds and ends.   If you were in the slightest degree a theologian, you would be neither surprised nor disconcerted at what I have just said.

"Diversity is hateful.   It is the characteristic of evil to be diverse.   This characteristic manifests itself in the government of the Republic, which is more alienated than any other from unity.   With its want of unity it fails in independence, permanence, and power.   It fails in knowledge, and one may say

of it that it knows not what it does.   Although for
our chastisement it continues, yet it has no continuity.
For the idea of continuity implies that of identity,
and the Republic of one day is never the same as
that of the day before.   Even its ugliness and its
vices do not belong to it.   And you have yourself
remarked that by them it has never been discredited.   Reproaches and scandals that would
have ruined the mightiest empire have poured
over it harmlessly.   It is indestructible, for it is
destruction.   It is dispersion, it is discontinuity, it
is diversity, it is evil."

M. BERGERET : "Are you speaking of Republics
in general, or only of our own ? "

M. LANTAIGNE : "Obviously I am considering
neither the Roman Republic, nor the Dutch, nor the
Swiss, but only the French.   For these governments
have nothing in common save the name, and you
will not charge me with judging them by the name
by which they call themselves, nor by those points
in which they seem, one and all, opposed to monarchy
—an opposition which is not in itself necessarily to be
condemned ; but the Republic in France means
nothing more than the lack of a prince and the
want of a governing power.   And this nation was
too old at the time of the amputation for one not to
fear that it would die of it."

M. BERGERET : " Yet France has already survived

the Empire by twenty-seven years, the *bourgeois*-king by forty-eight years, and the legitimate sovereign by sixty-six years."

M. LANTAIGNE : " Say rather that for a century France, wounded to death, has been dragging out a miserable remnant of life in alternate fits of fever and prostration.   And do not imagine that I flatter the past or base my regrets on lying pictures of an age of gold which never existed.   The conditions of national life are quite familiar to me.   Its hours are marked by perils, its days by disasters.   And it is just and necessary that it should be so.   Its life, like that of individual men, if it were exempt from trials, would have no meaning.   The early history of France is full of crimes and expiations.   God ceaselessly chastened this nation with the zeal of an untiring love, and in the time of the kings His mercy spared her no suffering.   But, being then Christian, her woes were useful and precious to her.   In them she recognised the ennobling power of chastisement.   From them she derived her lessons, her merits, her salvation, her power, and her renown. Now her sufferings have no longer any meaning for her ; she neither understands them nor acquiesces in them.   Whilst undergoing the test she rebels against it.   And the demented state expects good fortune !   It is in losing faith in God that one loses, along with the idea of the absolute, the knowledge of the relative and even the historic sense. God alone informs the logical sequence of human events which, without Him, would no longer follow one another in a rational and conceivable manner. And for the last hundred years the history of France has been an enigma for the French. Yet even in our days there was one solemn hour of hope and expectation.

"The horseman who rides forth at the hour appointed by God, and who is called now Shalmanezar, now Nebuchadnezzar, then Cyrus, Cambyses, Memmius, Titus, Alaric, Attila, Mahomet II., or William, had ridden with fiery trail across France. Humiliated, bleeding, and mutilated, she raised her eyes to Heaven. May that moment be counted to her for righteousness! She seemed to understand, and along with her faith to recover her intelligence, to recognise the value and the use of her vast and providential woes. She aroused her just men, her Christians, to form a sovereign assembly. Then appeared the spectacle of that assembly, renewing a solemn custom and consecrating France to the heart of Jesus. We saw, as in the times of Saint Louis, churches rising on the mountains, before the gaze of penitent cities ; we saw the foremost citizens preparing for the restoration of the monarchy."

M. BERGERET (*sotto voce*) : " 1. The Assembly of Bordeaux. 2. The Sacré-Cœur of Montmartre and the Church of Fourvières at Lyons.   3. The Commission of the Nine and the mission of M. Chesnelong."

M. LANTAIGNE : " What do you say ? "

M. BERGERET : " Nothing.   I am filling in the headings in the *Discours sur l'Histoire universelle*."

M. LANTAIGNE : " Do not jest and do not deny. Coming along the roads sounded the white horses that were bringing the king to his own again. Henri Dieudonné was coming to re-establish the principle of authority from which spring the two social forces : command and obedience ; he was coming to restore human order along with divine order, political wisdom along with the religious spirit, the hierarchy, law, discipline, true liberty and unity.   The nation, linking up its traditions once more, was recovering, along with the sense of its mission, the secret of its power and the pledge of victory. . . . God willed it not.   These great designs, thwarted by the enemy who still hated us after having satisfied his hatred, opposed by a great number of the French, miserably supported even by those who had formed them, were brought to naught in one day.   The frontier of our country was barricaded against Henri Dieudonné, and the people subsided into a Republic ; that is to say, they repudiated their birthright, they renounced their rights and their duties, in order to govern themselves according to

L

their own inclinations and to live at their ease in that liberty which God curbs and which overturns both law and order, the temporal images of Himself. Henceforth evil was king and proclaimed its edicts. The Church, exposed to incessant vexations, was perfidiously tempted on the one side to an impossible renunciation and on the other to revolt involving punishment."

M. BERGERET : "You doubtless reckon among the vexatious measures the expulsion of the fraternities ?"

M. LANTAIGNE : "It is clear that the expulsion of the fraternities was prompted by evil intentions, and was the result of malicious calculation. It is also certain that the religious who were expelled did not deserve such treatment. In striking them it was believed that the Church was being struck. But the blow, badly aimed, strengthened the body that they wished to shake, and restored to the parishes the authority and the resources which had been diverted from them. Our enemies did not know the Church, and their chief minister of that time, less ignorant than they, but more desirous of satisfying them than of destroying us, made a war on us that was merely mimic and for purposes of show. For I do not regard the expulsion of the non-licensed orders as an effective attack. Of course, I honour the victims of this clumsy persecution ; but

I consider that the Church of France has in the secular clergy a sufficient staff to govern and minister to souls without the help of the regulars.   Alas ! the Republic has inflicted deeper and more secret wounds on the Church.   You know too much about educational questions, Monsieur Bergeret, not to have discovered several of these plague-spots ; but the most poisonous one was induced by the introduction into the episcopate of priests feeble in mind or in character. . . . I have said enough about that.   The Christian at least consoles and reassures himself, knowing that the Church will not perish. But what will be the patriot's consolation ? He discovers that all the members of the State are gangrened and rotten.   In twenty years what progress in corruption ! A chief of the State whose sole virtue is his powerlessness, and who is denounced as criminal if it should get wind that he ventures to act, or even merely to think ; ministers subject to a foolish Parliament, which is believed to be corrupt, and whose members, more ignorant every day, were chosen, moulded, nominated in the godless clubs of the freemasons to carry out an evil policy of which they are yet incapable, and which is surpassed by the evils brought about through their turbulent inaction ; an incessantly increasing bureaucracy, vast, greedy, and mischievous, in which the Republic believes she is securing for herself a band of supporters, but

which she is nourishing to her own ruin ; a magistracy recruited without law or equity, and too often
canvassed by the government not to be suspected of
obsequiousness ; an army, nay, a whole nation, un-
ceasingly pervaded by the fatal spirit of independence
and equality, is poured back straightway into town and
country, a whole community, depraved by barrack
life, unfitted for arts and trades, and disliking all
labour ; an educational body which has a mission to
teach atheism and immorality ; a diplomatic corps
which fails in readiness and authority, and which
leaves the care of our foreign policy and the conclusion of our alliances to innkeepers, shopkeepers
and journalists ; in a word, all the powers, the legis-
lative and the executive, the judicial, the military, and
the civil, intermingled, confused, destroyed one by
the other ; a farcical rule which, in its destructive
weakness, has given to society the two most powerful instruments of death that wickedness ever
devised : divorce and malthusianism.   And all the
evils of which I have made a rapid summary belong
to the Republic and spring naturally from her : the
Republic is essentially unrighteous.   She is unrighteous in willing a liberty which God has not
willed, since He is the master, and since He has
delegated to priests and kings a part of his authority ;
she is unrighteous in willing an equality which God
has not willed, since He has established the hierarchy

of dignities in Heaven and on earth ; she is unrighteous in instituting that tolerance which cannot
be the will of God, since evil is intolerable ; she is
unrighteous in consulting the will of the people, as
if the multitude of ignorant ought to prevail against
the small company of those who bow themselves
before the will of God, which overshadows the
government and even the details of administration,
as a principle whose consequences are never-ending ;
in a word, she is unrighteous in proclaiming her
indifference to religion—that is to say, her impiety,
her unbelief, her blasphemies (of which the very
smallest is mortal sin), and her adhesion to diversity,
which is evil and death."

M. BERGERET : " Did you not say just now, monsieur l'abbé, that being as republican as the Pope,
you were resolved to live at peace with the Republic ? "

M. LANTAIGNE : " Certainly, I will live with her in
submission and obedience.   In rebelling against her,
I should act according to her principles, and contrary
to my own.   By being seditious I should resemble
her, and I should no longer resemble myself.

" It is unlawful to return evil for evil.   Sovereignty
is hers.   Whether she decrees ill or does not decree,
hers is the guilt.   Let it rest with her !   My duty
is to obey.   I shall do it.   I shall obey.   As a
priest and, if it please God, as a bishop, I shall

refuse nothing to the Republic of what I owe her.
I call to mind that Saint Augustine, in Hippo, then
besieged by the Vandals, died a bishop and a Roman
citizen. For myself, the lowest member of this
illustrious Church of the Gauls, after the example
of the greatest of the doctors, I will die in France,
a priest and a French citizen, praying God to scatter
the Vandals."

The elm-trees on the Mall began to incline their
shadow towards the east. A fresh breeze coming
from a region of distant storm stirred among the
leaves. Whilst a ladybird travelled over the sleeve
of his coat, M. Bergeret replied to Abbé Lantaigne
in a tone of the greatest affability.

"Monsieur l'abbé, you have just traced, with an
eloquence only to be found on your lips, the charac-
teristics of democratic rule. This government is
very much as you describe it. And yet it is the one
I prefer. In it all bonds are loosened, which weakens
the State, but relieves individuals and ensures a
certain ease of life and a liberty which unfortunately
local tyrannies counteract. It is true that corruption
appears to be greater in it than in monarchies. That
springs from the number and diversity of the people
who are raised to power. But this corruption would
be less visible if the secret of it were better kept.
The lack of secrecy and the want of continuity
render all enterprise impossible in a democratic

Republic.   But, since the enterprises of monarchies have most often ruined the nations, I am not very sorry to live under a government incapable of great designs.   What rejoices me especially in our Republic is the sincere desire which she shows not to provoke war in Europe.   She rejoices in militarism, but is not at all bellicose.   In considering the chances of a war, other governments have nothing to fear save defeat.   Ours fears equally—and justly so—both victory and defeat.   This salutary fear secures us peace, which is the greatest of blessings.

"The worst fault of the present *régime* is that it costs very dear.   It makes no outward show : it is not ostentatious.   It is gorgeous neither in its women nor its horses.   But, with its humble appearance and neglected exterior, it is expensive. It has too many poor relations, too many friends to provide for.   It is a spendthrift.   The most grievous point is that it lives on an exhausted country, whose powers are waning and which no longer thrives. And the administration has great need of money. It is aware that it is in difficulties.   And its difficulties are greater than it fancies.   They will increase still more.   The evil is not new.   It is the one which killed the old *régime*.   I am going, monsieur l'abbé, to tell you a great truth : as long as the State contents itself with the revenues supplied by the poor, as long as it has enough from the subsidies

which are assured to it with mechanical regularity
by those who work with their hands, it lives happy,
peaceful, and honoured. Economists and financiers
are pleased to acknowledge its honesty. But as soon
as this unhappy State, driven by need, makes a show
of asking for money from those who have it, and of
levying some slight toll on the rich, it is made to feel
that it is committing a horrible outrage, is violating
all rights, is wanting in respect to a sacred thing, is
destroying commerce and industry, and crushing the
poor by touching the rich. No one hides his conviction that discredit is at hand. And it sinks
beneath the genuine contempt of the good citizen.
Yet ruin comes slowly and surely. The State touches
capital : it is lost.

" Our ministers are jesting at us when they speak
of the clerical or the socialist peril. There is but
one peril, the financial peril. The Republic is
beginning to recognise this. I pity her, I shall
regret her. I was reared under the Empire, in love
for the Republic. 'She is justice,' my father, professor of rhetoric at the college of Saint-Omer, used
to say to me. He did not know her. She is not
justice, but she is ease. Monsieur l'abbé, if you
had a soul less exalted, less serious, and more given
to jesting thoughts, I should confide to you that the
present Republic, the Republic of 1896, delights me
and touches me by its modesty. She acquiesces in

not being admired. She exacts but a trifling respect, and even renounces esteem. It is enough for her to live. That is her sole desire; it is a lawful one. The humblest beings cling to life. Like the wood-cutter of the fabulist, like the apothecary of Mantua, who so greatly astonished that young fool of a Romeo, she fears death, and it is her only fear. She mistrusts princes and soldiers. In danger of death, she would be very ill to handle. Fear would make her abandon her own nature and would render her ferocious. That would be a pity. But as long as they make no attempt on her life, and as long as they only attack her honour, she is good-natured. A government of this kind suits me and gives me confidence. So many others were merciless through self-esteem! So many others made sure of their rights, their grandeur, and their prosperity by cruelties! So many others have poured out blood for their prerogative and their majesty! She has no self-esteem; she has no majesty. A fortunate lack which keeps her innocuous to us! Provided that she lives, she is content. She rules laxly, and I should be tempted to praise her for that more than for all the rest. And since she governs laxly, I forgive her for governing badly. I suspect men at all times of having much exaggerated the necessity of government and the benefits of a strong adminis-tration. Certainly strong administrations make nations great and prosperous. But the nations have suffered so much all through the centuries for their grandeur and prosperity, that I fancy they would renounce it. Glory has cost them too dear for them to resent the fact that our present rulers have only procured for us the colonial variety of it. If the uselessness of all government should at last be discovered, the Republic of M. Carnot would have paved the way for this priceless discovery. And one ought to feel some gratitude towards it for that. Taking everything into consideration, I feel much attached to our institutions."

Thus spoke M. Bergeret, professor of literature at the University.

Abbé Lantaigne rose, drew out from his pocket his blue-checkered handkerchief, passed it over his lips, returned it to his pocket, smiled, contrary to his custom, secured his breviary under his arm, and said :

" You express yourself pleasantly, Monsieur Bergeret. Just so did the rhetors talk in Rome when Alaric entered it with his Visigoths. Yet under the terebinth trees of the Esquiline the rhetors of the fifth century let fall thoughts of less vanity. For then Rome was Christian. You are that no longer."

" Monsieur l'abbé," replied the professor, " be a bishop and not the head of the University."

"It is true, Monsieur Bergeret," said the priest with a loud laugh, "that if I were head of the University I should forbid you to be a teacher of youth."

"And you would do me a great service. For then I should write in the papers, like M. Jules Lemaître, and who knows whether, like him . . ."

"Well! well! you would not be out of place among the wits. And the French Academy has a partiality for freethinkers."

He spoke and walked away with a firm, straight, heavy tread. M. Bergeret remained alone in the middle of the bench, which was now three-parts covered by shade. The ladybird which had been fluttering its wing-cases on his shoulder for a moment flew away. He began to dream. He was not happy, for he had an acute mind whose points were not always turned outwards, and very often he pricked himself with the needle-points of his own criticism. Anæmic and bilious, he had a very weak digestion and enfeebled senses, which brought him more disgust and suffering than pleasure and happiness. He was reckless in speech, and in un-erringness and precision his tactlessness attained the same results as the most practised skill. With cunning art he seized every opportunity of injuring himself. He inspired the majority of people with a natural aversion, and being sociable and inclined to fraternise with his fellows, he suffered from that fact. He had never succeeded in moulding his pupils, and he delivered his lectures on Latin literature in a gloomy, damp, deserted cellar, in which he was buried through the Dean's burning hatred of him. The University buildings were, however, spacious. Built in 1894, "these new premises," according to the words of M. Worms-Clavelin at the opening, "testified to the zeal of the government of the Republic for the diffusion of learning." They boasted an amphitheatre, decorated by M. Léon Glaize with allegorical paintings representing Science and Literature, where M. Compagnon gave his much-belauded lectures on mathematics. The other gownsmen in their red or yellow taught different subjects in handsome, well-lighted rooms. M. Bergeret alone, under the bedel's ironic glance, had to descend, followed by three students, into a dusky, subterranean hole. There, in the heavy, noisome air, he expounded the *Æneid* with German scholarship and French subtlety ; there, by his literary and moral pessimism, he afflicted M. Roux, of Bordeaux, his best pupil ; there, he opened up new vistas, whose aspect was terrifying ; there, one evening he pronounced those words now become famous, but which ought rather to have perished, stifled in the shadow of the vault : "Fragments of differing origins, soldered clumsily on to each other,

made up the *Iliad* and the *Odyssey*. Such are the
models of composition that have been imitated by
Virgil, by Fénelon, and in general, in classic litera-
tures, by writers of narratives in verse or in prose."

M. Bergeret was not happy. He had received no
honorary distinction. It is true that he despised
honours. But he felt that it would have been much
finer to despise them while accepting them. He
was obscure and less well known in the town for
works of talent than M. de Terremondre, author
of a Tourist Guide ; than General Milher, a distinguished miscellaneous writer of the department ;
less even than his pupil, M. Albert Roux, of Bordeaux,
author of *Nirée*, a poem in *vers libres*. Certainly he
despised literary fame, knowing that that of Virgil in
Europe rested on a double misconception, one absurd
and the other fabulous. But he suffered at having no
intercourse with writers who, like MM. Faguet,
Doumic, or Pellissier, seemed akin to him in mind.
He would have liked to know them, to live with
them in Paris, like them to write in reviews, to
contradict, to rival, perhaps to outstrip them. He
recognised in himself a certain subtlety of intellect,
and he had written pages which he knew to be
pleasing.

He was not happy. He was poor, shut up with
his wife and his three daughters in a little dwelling,
where he tasted to the full the inconveniences of

domestic life ; and it harassed him to find hair-
curlers on his writing-table, and to see the margins
of his manuscripts singed by curling-tongs.   The
only secure and pleasant place of retreat that he had
in the world was that bench on the Mall shaded by
an ancient elm, and the old-book corner in Paillot's
shop.

He meditated for a moment on his sad condition ;
then he rose from his bench and took the road which
leads to the bookseller's.

XIV

WHEN M. Bergeret entered the shop, Paillot, the bookseller, with a pencil thrust behind his ear, was collecting his "returns." He was stacking up the volumes whose yellow covers, after long exposure to the sunlight, had turned brown and become covered with fly-marks. These were the unsaleable copies, which he was sending back to the publishers. M. Bergeret recognised among the "returns" several works that he liked. He felt no chagrin at this, having too much taste to hope to see his favourite authors winning the votes of the crowd.

He sank down, as he was accustomed to do, in the old-book corner, and through mere habit took up the thirty-eighth volume of *l'Histoire Générale des Voyages*. The book, bound in green leather, opened of its own accord at p. 212, and M. Bergeret once more read these fatal lines :

" a passage to the North. 'It is to this check,' said he, ' that we owe the opportunity of being able to visit the Sandwich Isles again . . .'"

And M. Bergeret sank into melancholy.

M. Mazure, the archivist of the department, and M. de Terremondre, president of the Society of Agriculture and Archæology, who both had their rush-bottomed chairs in the old-book corner, came in opportunely to join the professor. M. Mazure was a paleographer of great merit. But his manners were not elegant. He had married the servant of the archivist, his predecessor, and appeared in the town in a straw hat with battered crown. He was a radical, and published documents concerning the history of the county town during the Revolution. He enjoyed inveighing against the royalists of the department ; but having applied for academic honours without having received them, he began invectives against his political friends, and particularly against M. Worms-Clavelin, the *préfet*.

Being insulting by nature, his professional practice of discovering secrets disposed him to slander and calumny. Nevertheless he was good company, especially at table, where he used to sing drinking songs.

"You know," said he to M. de Terremondre and M. Bergeret, "that the *préfet* uses the house of Rondonneau junior for assignations with women. He has been caught there. Abbé Guitrel also haunts the place. And, appropriately enough, the house is called, in a land-survey of 1783, the House of the Two Satyrs."

"But," said M. de Terremondre, "there are no women of loose life in the house of Rondonneau junior."

"They are taken there," answered Mazure, the archivist.

"Talking of that," said M. de Terremondre, "I have heard, my dear Monsieur Bergeret, that you have been shocking my old friend Lantaigne, on the Mall, by a cynical confession of your political and social immorality. They say that you know neither law nor curb . . ."

"They are mistaken," replied M. Bergeret.

". . . that you are indifferent in the matter of government."

"Not at all! But, to tell the truth, I do not attach any special importance to the form of the State. Changes of government make little change in the condition of individuals. We do not depend on constitutions or on charters, but on instincts and morals. It serves no purpose at all to change the name of public necessities. And it is only the crazy and the ambitious who make revolutions."

"It is not above ten years ago," replied M. Mazure, "that I would have risked a broken head for the Republic. To-day I could see her turn a somersault, and only laugh and cross my arms. The old republicans are despised. Favour is only granted to the turncoats. I am not referring to you, Monsieur

M

de Terremondre. But I am disgusted. I have come to think with M. Bergeret. All governments are ungrateful."

" They are all powerless," said M. Bergeret ; "and I have here in my pocket a little tale which I should very much like to read to you. I have founded it on an anecdote which my father often related to me. It proves that absolute power is powerlessness itself. I should like to have your opinion on this trifle. If you do not disapprove of it, I shall send it to the *Revue de Paris*."

M. de Terremondre and M. Mazure drew their chairs up to that of M. Bergeret, who pulled a note-book from his pocket and began to read in a weak, but clear voice :

A DEPUTY MAGISTRATE

In a salon of the Tuileries the ministers had assembled . . .

" Allow me to listen," said M. Paillot, the bookseller. " I am waiting for Léon, who is not back yet. When he is out, he never comes back. I am obliged to tend the shop and serve the customers. But I shall hear at least a part of the reading. I like to improve my mind."

" Very well, Paillot," said M. Bergeret, and he resumed :

A DEPUTY MAGISTRATE

In a salon of the Tuileries the ministers had assembled in council, under the presidency of the Emperor.   Napoleon III. was silently making marks with a pencil on a plan of an industrial town.   His long, sallow face, with its melancholy sweetness, had a strange appearance amid the square heads of the men of affairs and the bronzed faces of the men of toil. He half raised his eyelids, glanced with his gentle, vague look round the oval table, and asked :

"Gentlemen, is there any other matter to be discussed ?"

His voice issued from his thick moustaches a little muffled and hollow, and seemed to come from very far off.

At this moment the Keeper of the Seals made a sign to his colleague of the Home Department which the latter did not seem to notice.—At that time the Keeper of the Seals was M. Delarbre, a magistrate in virtue of his birth, who had displayed in his high judicial functions a becoming pliability, abruptly laid aside now and then for the rigidity of a profes- sional dignity that nothing could bend.   It was said that, after having become an ultramontane and a member of the Empress's party, the jansenism of those great lawyers, his ancestors, sometimes bubbled up in his nature.   But those who had access to him

considered him to be merely punctilious, a trifle
fanciful, indifferent to the great questions which his
mind did not grasp, and obstinate about the trifles
which suited the pettiness of his intriguing character.

The Emperor was preparing to rise, with his two
hands on the gilt arms of his chair. Delarbre, seeing
that the Home Secretary, his nose in his papers,
was avoiding his look, took it upon himself to
challenge him.

"Pardon me, my dear colleague, for raising a
question which, although it started in your department, none the less concerns mine. But you have
yourself declared to me your intention of apprising
the Council of the extremely delicate situation in
which a magistrate has been placed by the *préfet* of a
department in the West."

The Home Secretary shrugged his broad shoulders
slightly and looked at Delarbre with some im-
patience. He had the air, at once jovial and choleric,
which belongs to great demagogues.

"Oh," said he, "that was gossip, ridiculous tittle-
tattle, a rumour which I should be ashamed to bring
to the notice of the Emperor, were it not that my
colleague, the Minister of Justice, seems to attach
an importance to it which, for my part, I have not
succeeded in discovering."

Napoleon began sketching once more. "It has
to do with the *préfet* of Loire-Inférieure," continued

the minister. "This official is reputed, in his department, to be a gallant squire of dames, and the reputation for gallantry which has become attached to his name, combined with his well-known courtesy and his devotion to the government, has contributed not a little to the popularity which he enjoys in the country. His attentions to Madame Méreau, the wife of the *procureur-général*, have been noticed and commented on. I grant that M. Pélisson, the *préfet*, has given occasion for scandalous gossip in Nantes, and that severe charges have been laid to his account in the bourgeois circles of the county town, especially in the drawing-rooms frequented by the magistracy. Assuredly M. Pélisson's attitude towards Madame Méreau, whose position ought to have protected her from any such equivocal attentions, would be regrettable, if it were continued. But the information I have received enables me to state that Madame Méreau has not been actually compromised and that no scandal is to be anticipated. A little prudence and circumspection will suffice to prevent this affair having any annoying consequences."

Having spoken in these terms, the Home Secretary closed his portfolio and leant back in his chair.

The Emperor said nothing.

"Excuse me, my dear colleague!" said the Keeper of the Seals drily, "the wife of the *procureur-*

général of the court of Nantes is the mistress of the *préfet* of Loire-Inférieure; this connection, known throughout the whole district, is calculated to injure the prestige of the magistracy. It is important to call the attention of His Majesty to this state of things."

"Doubtless," replied the Home Secretary, his gaze turned towards the allegories on the ceiling, "doubtless, such facts are to be regretted; yet one must in no way exaggerate; it is possible that the *préfet* of Loire-Inférieure may have been a little imprudent and Madame Méreau a little giddy, but . . ."

The minister wafted the rest of his ideas towards the mythological figures which floated across the painted sky. There was a moment's silence, during which one could hear the impudent chirping of the sparrows perched on the trees in the garden and on the eaves of the château.

M. Delarbre bit his thin lips and pulled his austere but coquettish moustaches. He replied:

"Excuse my persistence; the secret reports which I have received leave no doubt as to the nature of the relationship between M. Pélisson and Madame Méreau. These relations were already established two years ago. In fact, in the month of September 18— the *préfet* of Loire-Inférieure got the *procureur-général* an invitation to hunt with the Comte de

Morainville, deputy for the third division in the department, and during the magistrate's absence he entered Madame Méreau's room. He got in by way of the kitchen-garden. The next day the gardener saw traces that the wall had been scaled and informed the police. Inquiry was made ; they even arrested a tramp, who, not being able to prove his innocence, endured several months of precautionary imprisonment. He had, it is true, a very bad record and no special points of interest about him. Still to this day the *procureur-général* persists, supported by a very small proportion of the public, in believing him to be guilty of house-breaking. The position, I repeat, is rendered by this fact no less annoying and prejudicial to the prestige of the magistracy."

The Home Secretary poured over the discussion, according to his wont, certain massive phrases calculated to close and suppress it by their weight. He held, said he, his *préfets* in the palm of his hand ; he would be able to lead M. Pélisson easily to a just appreciation of things, without taking any drastic measure against an intelligent and zealous official, who had succeeded in his department, and who was valuable " from the point of view of the electoral position." No one could say that he was more interested than the Home Secretary in maintaining a good understanding between the officials of the departments and the judicial authority.

Still the Emperor kept that dreamy look in which he was usually wrapped when silent.   He was evidently thinking of past events, for he suddenly said : " Poor M. Pélisson !   I knew his father.   He was called Anacharsis Pélisson.   He was the son of a republican of 1792 ; himself a republican, he used to write in the opposition papers during the July administration.   At the time of my captivity in the fortress of Ham, he addressed a friendly letter to me.   You cannot imagine the joy which the slightest token of sympathy gives a prisoner.   After that we went on our separate paths.   We never saw one another again.   He is dead."

The Emperor lit a cigarette and remained wrapped in his dream for a moment.   Then rising :

" Gentlemen, I will not detain you."

With the awkward gait of a great winged bird when it walks, he returned to his private apartments ; and the ministers went out, one after the other, through the long suite of rooms, beneath the solemn gaze of the ushers.   The marshal who was the Minister of War held out his cigar-case to the Keeper of the Seals.

" Monsieur Delarbre, shall we take a little walk outside ?   I want to stretch my legs."

Whilst they were both walking down the Rue de Rivoli, by the railing that borders the Terrasse des Feuillants :

" Speaking of cigars," said the marshal, " I only like very dry one-sou cigars. The others seem like sweetmeats to me. Don't you know . . ."

He cut short his thought, then :

" This Pélisson that you were talking about just now in the Council, isn't he a little dried up, swarthy man, who was *sous-préfet* at Saint-Dié five years ago ?"

Delarbre replied that Pélisson had indeed been *sous-préfet* in the Vosges.

" So I said to myself : I knew Pélisson. And I remember Madame Pélisson very well. I sat next to her at dinner at Saint-Dié, when I went there for the unveiling of a monument. Don't you know . . ."

" What kind of woman is she ? " asked Delarbre.

" Tiny, swarthy, thin. A deceptive thinness. In the morning, in a high-necked dress, she looked a mere wisp. At table in the evening, in a low-necked dress with flowers in her bosom, very charming."

" But morally, marshal ? "

" Morally. . . . I am not an imbecile, am I, now ? Well ! I have never understood anything about a woman's morals. All that I can tell you is that Madame Pélisson passed for a sentimentalist. They said she had a warm heart for handsome men."

" She gave you a hint to that effect, my dear marshal ? "

" Not the least in the world. She said to me at dessert, 'I dote on eloquence. A noble speech

carries me away.'   I could not apply that remark to
myself.   It is true that I had that morning delivered
an address.   But I had got my aide-de-camp, a short-
sighted artillery officer, to write it out for me.   He
had written so small that I could not read it. . . .
Don't you know ? . . ."

They had reached the Place Vendôme.   Delarbre
held out his little withered hand to the marshal, and
stole under the archway of the Ministry.

*   *   *   *   *

The following week, at the breaking up of the
Council, when the ministers were already withdraw-
ing, the Emperor laid his hand on the shoulder of
the Keeper of the Seals.

"My dear Monsieur Delarbre," said he to him,
" I have heard by chance—in my position, one never
learns anything save by chance—that there is a deputy
magistrate's post vacant at the Nantes bar.   I beg
that you will consider for that post a very deserving
young doctor of law, who has written a remarkable
treatise on Trade Unions.   His name is Chanot, and
he is the nephew of Madame Ramel.   He is to
beg an audience of you this very day.   Should you
propose him to me for it, I shall sign his nomination
with pleasure."

The Emperor had pronounced the name of his
foster-sister tenderly, for he had never lost his

affection for her, although, a republican of republicans, she repelled his advances, refused, poor widow as she was, the master's offers, and raged openly in her garret against the *coup d'état*. But yielding at last, after fifteen years, to the persistent kindness of Napoleon III., she had come to beg, as earnest of reconciliation, a favour from the prince—not for herself, but for her nephew young Chanot, a doctor of law, and, according to his professors, an honour to the Schools. Even now it was an austere favour that Madame Ramel demanded of her foster-brother ; admission to the open court for young Chanot could scarcely be considered an act of partiality. But Madame Ramel was keenly anxious that her nephew should be sent to Loire-Inférieure, where his relatives lived. This fact recurred to Napoleon's mind, and he impressed it on the Minister of Justice.

"It is very important," said he, "that my candidate should be nominated at Nantes, for that is his native place and where his parents live. That is an important consideration for a young man whose means are small and who likes family life."

"Chanot . . . hard-working, meritorious, and with small means . . ." answered the minister.

He added that he would use his best endeavours to act in accordance with the desire expressed by His Majesty. His only fear was lest the *procureur-général* should have already submitted to him a list of proposed nominees, among whom, naturally, the name Chanot would not occur. This *procureur-général* was, indeed, M. Méreau, concerning whom there had been a discussion in the preceding Council. The Keeper of the Seals was particularly anxious to act very handsomely towards him. But he would strain every nerve to bring this affair to an issue that conformed with the intentions expressed by His Majesty.

He bowed and took his leave. It was his reception day. As soon as he had entered his study, he asked his secretary, Labarthe, whether there were many people in the ante-room. There were two presidents of courts, a councillor of the Appeal Court, the Cardinal-Archbishop of Nicomedia, a crowd of judges, barristers, and priests. The minister asked if there was any one there called Chanot. Labarthe searched in the silver salver, and discovered, among the pile of cards, that of Chanot, doctor of law, prizeman of the Faculty of Law, Paris. The minister ordered him to be called first, merely requesting that he should be conducted by the back passages, in order not to offend the magistrates and clergy.

The minister seated himself at his table and murmured quite to himself:

"'A sentimentalist,' said the marshal, 'with a warm heart for handsome men who speak well.' . . ."

The usher introduced into the study a huge, tall young man, stooping, spectacled, and with a pointed skull.   Every part of his uncouth frame expressed at once the timidity of the recluse and the boldness of the thinker.

The Keeper of the Seals examined him from head to foot and saw that he had the cheeks of a child and no shoulders.   He signed to him to sit down. The suitor, having perched himself at the edge of the chair, shut his eyes and began to pour forth a flood of words.

" Monsieur *le Ministre*, I come to beg from your noble patronage the privilege of admission to the magistracy.   Possibly Your Excellence may consider that the reports I have gained in the various examinations which I have undergone, and a prize which has been awarded to me for a work on Trade Unions, are sufficient qualifications, and that the nephew of Madame Ramel, foster-sister of the Emperor, is not altogether unworthy . . ."

The Keeper of the Seals stopped him with a wave of his little yellow hand.

" Doubtless, Monsieur Chanot, doubtless an august patronage, which would never have been mistakenly bestowed on an unworthy recipient, has been secured for you.   I know it, the Emperor takes much interest in you.   You desire a chair as judge-advocate, Monsieur Chanot ? "

" Your Excellence," replied Chanot, " would put the finishing touch to my wishes by nominating me deputy magistrate at Nantes, where my family live."

Delarbre fixed his leaden eyes on Chanot and said drily :

" There is no vacancy at the bar of Nantes."

" Excuse me, Your Excellency, I thought . . ."

The minister rose.

" There is none there."

And whilst Chanot was making clumsily for the door and looking for an exit in the white panels as he made his bow, the Keeper of the Seals said to him, with a persuasive air and almost in a confidential tone :

" Trust me, Monsieur Chanot, and dissuade your aunt from making any new solicitations which, far from being of any profit to you, will only do you harm.   Rest assured that the Emperor takes an interest in you, and rely on me."

As soon as the door was shut the minister called his secretary.

" Labarthe, bring me your candidate."

＊   ＊   ＊   ＊   ＊

At eight o'clock in the evening Labarthe entered a house in the Rue Jacob, mounted the staircase as far as the attics, and called from the landing :

"Are you ready, Lespardat?"

The door of a little garret opened. Inside on a shelf there were several law-books and tattered novels; on the bed a black velvet mask with a fall of lace, a bunch of withered violets, and some fencing foils. On the wall a bad portrait of Mirabeau, a copper-plate engraving. In the middle of the room a big bronzed fellow was brandishing dumb-bells. He had frizzled hair, a low forehead, hazel eyes full of laughter and sweetness, a nose that quivered like the nostrils of a horse, and in his pleasantly gaping mouth strong white teeth.

"I was waiting for you," said he.

Labarthe begged him to dress himself. He was hungry. What time would they get their dinner?

Lespardat, having laid his dumb-bells on the floor, pulled off his jersey, and showed the herculean nape that carried his round head on his broad shoulders.

"He looks at least twenty-six," thought Labarthe.

As soon as Lespardat had put on his coat, the thin cloth of which allowed one to follow the powerful, easy play of the muscles, Labarthe pushed him outside.

"We shall be at Magny's in three minutes. I have the minister's brougham."

As they had matters to discuss, they asked for a private room at the restaurant.

After the sole and the *pré-salé*, Labarthe attacked his subject bluntly :

"Listen to me carefully, Lespardat. You will see my chief to-morrow, your nomination will be proposed by the *procureur-général* of Nantes on Thursday, and on Monday submitted for the signature of the Emperor. It is arranged that it shall be given to him unexpectedly, at the moment when he will be busy with Alfred Maury in fixing the site of Alesia. When he is studying the topography of the Gauls in the time of Cæsar, the Emperor signs everything they want him to. But understand clearly what is expected from you. You must win the favour of Madame *la préfète*. You must win from her the ultimate favour. It is only by this consummation that the magistracy will be avenged."

Lespardat swallowed and listened, pleased and smiling in his ingenuous self-conceit.

"But," said he, "what notion has budded in Delarbre's head ? I thought he was a puritan."

Labarthe, raising his knife, stopped him.

"First of all, my friend, I beg that you will not compromise my chief, who must remain ignorant of all that's going on here. But since you have brought in Delarbre's name, I will tell you that his puritanism is a jansenist puritanism. He is a great-nephew of Deacon Pâris. His maternal great-uncle was that M. Carré de Montgeron who defended the fanatics of Saint-Médard's Cloister * before the Parliament. Now the jansenists love to practise their austerities in nooks and crannies ; they have a taste for diplomatic and canonical blackguardism. It is the effect of their perfect purity. And then they read the Bible. The Old Testament is full of stories of the same kind as yours, my dear Lespardat."

Lespardat was not listening. He was floating in a sea of naïve delight. He was asking himself : " What will father say ? What will mother say ? " thinking of his parents, grocers of large ambitions and little wealth at Agen. And he vaguely associated his budding fortune with the glory of Mirabeau, his favourite hero. Since his college days he had dreamt of a destiny rich with women and feats of oratory.

Labarthe recalled his young friend's attention to himself.

" You know, monsieur *le substitut*, you are not irremovable. If after a reasonable interval you have not made yourself very agreeable to Madame Pélisson—I mean completely agreeable—you fall into disgrace."

---

* In 1730 miracles were claimed by the jansenists to have been worked in the cemetery of St. Médard, Paris, at the grave of François de Pâris, a young jansenist deacon. The spot became a place of pilgrimage, and was visited by thousands of jansenist fanatics.

"But," asked Lespardat frankly, "how much time do you give me to make myself excessively pleasing to Madame Pélisson ? "

"Until the vacation," answered the minister's secretary gravely. "We give you, in addition, all sorts of facilities, secret missions, furloughs, &c. Everything except money. Above all, we are an honest administration. People don't believe it. But later on they will find that we were no jobbers. Take Delarbre : he has clean hands. Besides, the Home Office, which is on the husband's side, controls the Secret Service Money. Do not count on anything save your two thousand four hundred francs of salary and your handsome face to captivate Madame Pélisson."

"Is she pretty, this *préfète* of mine ? " demanded Lespardat.

He asked this question carelessly, without exaggerating the importance of it, placidly, as behoves a very young man who finds all women beautiful. By way of reply, Labarthe threw on the table the photograph of a thin lady in a round hat, with a double bandeau falling on her brown neck.

"Here," said he, " is the portrait of Madame Pélisson. It was ordered by the Cabinet from the Prefecture of Police, and they sent it on after they had stamped it with a warranty stamp, as you see."

Lespardat seized it eagerly with his square fingers.

"She is handsome," said he.

"Have you a plan?" asked Labarthe. "A methodical scheme of operations."

"No," answered Lespardat simply.

Labarthe, who was keen-witted, protested that it was, however, necessary to foresee, to arrange, not to allow oneself to be taken unawares by any contingencies.

"You are certain," added he, "to be invited to the balls at the prefecture, and you will, of course, dance with Madame Pélisson. Do you know how to dance? Show me how you dance."

Lespardat rose, and, clasping his chair in his arms, took one turn of a waltz with the deportment of a graceful bear.

Labarthe watched him very gravely through his eyeglass.

"You are heavy, awkward, without that irresistible suppleness which . . ."

"Mirabeau danced badly," said Lespardat.

"After all," said Labarthe, "perhaps it is only that the chair does not inspire you."

When they were both once more on the damp pavement of the narrow Rue Contrescarpe, they met several girls who were coming and going between the Carrefour Buci and the wine-shops of the Rue Dauphine. As one of these, a thick-set, heavy girl, in a dingy black dress, was passing sadly by under a street lamp with slack gait, Lespardat seized her roughly by the waist, lifted her, and made her take with him two turns of a waltz across the greasy pavement and into the gutter, before she had any idea what was happening.

Recovering from her astonishment, she shrieked the foulest insults at her cavalier, who carried her away with irresistible verve. He himself supplied the orchestra, in a baritone voice, as warm and seductive as military music, and whirled so madly with the girl that, all bespattered with mud and water from the street, they collided with the shafts of prowling cabs and felt on their neck the breath of the horses. After a few turns, she murmured in the young man's ear, her head sunk on his breast and all her anger gone :

" After all, you are a pretty fellow, you are. You ought to make them happy, didn't you ?—those girls at Bullier's."

" That's enough, my friend," cried Labarthe. " Don't go and get run in. My word, you will avenge the magistracy ! "

*   *   *   *   *

In the golden light of a September day four months later, the Minister of Justice and Religion, passing with his secretary under the arcades of the Rue de Rivoli, recognised M. Lespardat, the deputy magistrate of Nantes, at the very moment when the young man was hurrying into the Hôtel du Louvre.

"Labarthe," asked the minister, "did you know that your protégé was in Paris? Has he then nothing to keep him in Nantes? It seems to me that it is now some time since you have given me any confidential information about him. His start interested me, but I don't know yet whether he has quite lived up to the high opinion you formed of him."

Labarthe took up the cudgels for the *substitut;* he reminded the minister that Lespardat was on regular leave ; that at Nantes he had immediately gained the confidence of his chiefs at the bar, and that he had at the same time won the good graces of the *préfet.*

"M. Pélisson," added he, "cannot get on without him. It is Lespardat who organises the concerts at the prefecture."

Then the minister and his secretary continued their walk towards the Rue de la Paix, along the arcades, stopping here and there before the windows of the photograph shops.

"There are too many nude figures exposed in these shop-fronts," said the minister. "It would be better to take away their license from these shops. Strangers judge us by appearances, and such spectacles as these are calculated to injure the good name of the country and the government."

Suddenly, at the corner of the Rue de l'Échelle, Labarthe told his chief to look at a veiled woman who was coming towards them with a rapid step. But Delarbre, glancing at her for a moment, considered her very ordinary, far too slender, and not at all elegant.

"She is clumsily shod," said he; "she is from the provinces."

When she had passed them:

"Your Excellency is quite right," said Labarthe. "That is Madame Pélisson."

At this name the minister, much interested, turned round eagerly. With a vague feeling of his own dignity, he dared not follow her. But he showed his curiosity in his look.

Lebarthe spurred it on.

"I'll wager, monsieur *le ministre*, that she won't go very far."

They both hastened their steps, and saw Madame Pélisson follow the arcades, skirt the Place du Palais-Royal, and then, throwing uneasy glances to left and right, disappear into the Hôtel du Louvre.

At that the minister began to laugh from the depths of his throat. His little leaden eyes lighted up. And he muttered between his teeth the words which his secretary guessed rather than heard:

"The magistracy is avenged."

      *   *   *   *   *

On the same day the Emperor, then in residence at Fontainebleau, was smoking cigarettes in the library of the palace. He was leaning motionless, with the air of a melancholy sea-bird, against the case in which is kept the Monaldeschi coat of mail. Viollet-le-Duc and Mérimée, both his intimate friends, stood by his side.

He asked :

"Why, Monsieur Mérimée, do you like the works of Brantôme ?"

"Sire," replied Mérimée, "in them I recognise the French nation, with her good and bad qualities. She is never worse than when she is without a leader to show her a noble aim."

"Really," said the Emperor, "does one find that in Brantôme ?"

"One also finds in him," answered Mérimée, "the influence of women in the affairs of state."

At that moment Madame Ramel entered the gallery. Napoleon had given orders that she should be allowed to come to him whenever she presented herself. At the sight of his foster-sister he showed as much delight as his expressionless, sorrowful face was capable of displaying.

"My dear Madame Ramel," asked he, "how is your nephew getting on at Nantes ? Is he satisfied ?"

"But, sire," said Madame Ramel, "he was not sent there. Another was nominated in his place."

"That's strange," murmured His Majesty thoughtfully.

Then, placing his hand on the academician's shoulder :

"My dear Monsieur Mérimée, I am supposed to rule the fate of France, of Europe, and of the world. And I cannot get a nomination for a *substitut* of the sixth class, at a salary of two thousand four hundred francs."

XV

AVING finished his reading, M. Bergeret folded up his manuscript and put it in his pocket. M. Mazure, M. Paillot, and M. de Terremondre nodded three times in silence.

Then the last-named placed a hand on Bergeret's shoulder :

"What you have just read to us, my dear sir," said he, "is truly . . ."

At this moment Léon flung himself into the shop and exclaimed with a mixture of excitement and importance :

"Madame Houssieu has just been found strangled in her bed."

"How extraordinary !" said M. de Terremondre.

"From the state of the body," added Léon, "it is believed that death took place three days ago."

"Then," remarked M. Mazure, the archivist, "that would make it Saturday that the crime was committed."

Paillot, the bookseller, who had remained silent

up till now, with his mouth wide open out of deference to death, now began to collect his thoughts.

" On Saturday, about five o'clock in the afternoon, I plainly heard stifled cries and the heavy thud produced by the fall of a body. I even said to these gentlemen " (he turned towards M. de Terremondre and M. Bergeret) " that something extraordinary was going on in Queen Marguerite's house."

No one supported the claim that the bookseller was making that he alone, by the keenness of his senses and the penetration of his mind, had suspected the deed at the moment when it was taking place.

After a respectful silence, Paillot began again :

" During the night between Saturday and Sunday I said to Madame Paillot : ' There isn't a sound from Queen Marguerite's house.' "

M. Mazure asked the age of the victim. Paillot replied that Madame Houssieu was between seventy-nine and eighty years of age, that she had been a widow fifty years, that she owned landed property, stocks and shares, and a large sum of money, but that, being miserly and eccentric, she kept no servant, and cooked her victuals herself over the fireplace in her room, living alone amidst a wreckage of furniture and crockery, covered with the dust of a quarter of a century. It was actually more than twenty-five years since any one had wielded a broom in Queen Marguerite's house. Madame Houssieu went out but seldom, bought a whole week's supply of provisions for herself, and never let any one into the house save the butcher-boy and two or three urchins who ran errands for her.

"And the crime is supposed to have been committed on Saturday afternoon ?" asked M. de Terremondre.

"So it is believed, from the state of the body," replied Léon.   "It appears that it is a ghastly sight."

"On Saturday, in the afternoon," replied M. de Terremondre, "we were here, merely separated by a wall from the horrible scene, and we were chatting about passing trifles."

There was again a long silence.   Then some one asked if the assassin had been arrested, or if they even knew who it was.   But, in spite of his zeal, Léon could not answer these questions.

A shadow, which grew ever deeper and deeper and seemed funereal, began to fall across the bookseller's shop.   It was caused by the dark crowd of sightseers swarming in the square in front of the house of crime.

"Doubtless they are waiting for the inspector of police and the public prosecutor," said Mazure, the archivist.

Paillot, who was gifted with an exquisite caution, fearing lest the eager people would break the windowpanes, ordered Léon to close the shutters.

"Don't leave anything open," said he, "save the window which looks on the Rue des Tintelleries."

This precautionary measure seemed to bear the stamp of a certain moral delicacy. The gentlemen of the old-book corner approved of it. But since the Rue des Tintelleries was narrow, and since on that side the panes were covered with notices and drawing-copies, the shop became plunged in darkness.

The murmur of the crowd, till then unnoticed, spread with the shadow and became continuous, hollow, solemn, almost terrible, evidencing the unanimity of the moral condemnation.

Much moved, M. de Terremondre gave fresh expression to the thought which had struck him :

"It is strange," said he, "that while the crime was being committed so near us, we were talking quietly of unimportant affairs."

At this M. Bergeret bent his head towards his left shoulder, gave a far-away glance, and spoke thus:

"My dear sir, allow me to tell you that there is nothing strange in that. It is not customary, when a criminal action is going on, that conversations should stop of their own accord around the victim, either within a radius of so many leagues or even of so many feet. A commotion inspired by the most villainous thought only produces natural effects."

M. de Terremondre made no reply to this speech,

and the rest of his hearers turned away from M. Bergeret with a vague sense of disquietude and disapproval.

Still the professor of literature persisted :

" And why should an act so natural and so common as murder produce strange and uncommon results ? To kill is common to animals, and especially to man. Murder was for long ages regarded in human civilisation as a courageous action, and there still remain in our morals and institutions certain traces of this ancient point of view."

" What traces ? " demanded M. de Terremondre.

" They are to be found in the honours," replied M. Bergeret, " which are paid to soldiers."

" That is not the same thing," said M. de Terremondre.

" Certainly it is," said M. Bergeret. " For the motive force of all human actions is hunger or love. Hunger taught savages murder, impelled them to wars, to invasions. Civilised nations are like hunting-dogs. A perverted instinct drives them to destroy without profit or reason. The unreasonableness of modern wars disguises itself under dynastic interest, nationality, balance of power, honour. This last pretext is perhaps the most extravagant of all, for there is not a nation in the world that is not sullied with every crime and loaded with every shame. There is not one of them which has not endured all the humiliations that fortune could inflict on a miserable band of men. If there yet remains any honour among the nations, it is a strange means of upholding it to make war—that is to say, to commit all the crimes by which an individual dishonours himself : arson, robbery, rape, murder. And as for the actions whose motive power is love, they are for the most part as violent, as frenzied, as cruel as the actions inspired by hunger ; so much so that one must come to the conclusion that man is a mischievous beast. But it still remains to inquire why I know this, and whence it comes that the fact arouses grief and in- dignation in me. If nothing but evil existed, it would not be visible, as the night would have no name if the sun never rose."

M. de Terremondre, however, had extended enough deference to the religion of tenderness and human dignity by reproaching himself with having conversed in a gay and careless fashion at the moment of the crime and so near the victim. He began to regard the tragic end of Madame Houssieu as a familiar incident which one might look at straightforwardly and of which one might deduce the consequences. He reflected that now there was nothing to prevent his buying Queen Marguerite's house as a storehouse for his collections of furniture, china, and tapestry, and thus starting a sort of municipal museum. As a reward for his zeal and munificence, he counted on receiving, along with the applause of his fellow-countrymen, the Cross of the Legion of Honour, and perhaps the title of correspondent of the Institute.

He had in the Academy of Inscriptions two or three comrades, old bachelors like himself, with whom he sometimes lunched in Paris in some wine-shop, and to whom he recounted many anecdotes about women. And there was no correspondent for the district.

Hence he had already reached the point of depreciating the coveted house.

"It won't stand upright much longer," said he, "that house of Queen Marguerite. The beams of the floors used to fall in flakes of touchwood on the poor old octogenarian. It will be necessary to spend an immense sum in putting it in repair."

"The best thing," said Mazure, the archivist, "would be to pull it down and remove the frontage to the courtyard of the museum. It would really be a pity to abandon Philippe Tricouillard's shield to the wreckers."

They heard a great commotion among the crowd in the square. It was the noise of the people whom the police were driving back to clear a passage for the magistrates into the house of crime.

Paillot pushed his nose out of the half-open door.

"Here," said he, "comes the examining judge,

M. Roquincourt, with M. Surcouf, his clerk. They have gone into the house."

One after the other the academicians of the old-book corner had slipped out behind the bookseller on to the pavement of the Rue des Tintelleries, from which they watched the surging movements of the people who crowded the Place Saint-Exupère.

Among the mob Paillot recognised M. Cassignol, the president in chief. The old man was taking his daily constitutional. The excited crowd, in which he had got entangled during his walk, impeded his short steps and feeble sight. He went on, still upright and sturdy, carrying his withered, white head erect.

When Paillot saw him, he ran up to him, doffed his velvet cap, and, offering him his arm, invited him to come and sit down in the shop.

"How imprudent of you, Monsieur Cassignol, to venture into such a crowd! It's almost like a riot."

At the word riot, the old man had a vision, as it were, of the century of revolution, three parts of which he had seen. He was now in his eighty-seventh year, and had already been on the retired list for twenty-five years.

Leaning on the bookseller, Paillot, he crossed the doorstep of the shop and sat down on a rush-bottomed chair, in the midst of the respectful academicians. His malacca cane, with its silver top, trembled under his hand between his hollow thighs. His spine was stiffer than the back of his chair. He drew off his tortoiseshell spectacles to wipe them, and it took him a long time to put them on again. He had lost his memory for faces, and although he was hard of hearing, it was by the voice that he recognised people.

He asked concisely for the cause of the crowds which had gathered in the square, but he hardly listened to the answer given him by M. de Terremondre. His brain, sound but ossified, steeped as it were in myrrh, received no new impressions, although old ideas and passions remained deeply embedded in it.

MM. de Terremondre, Mazure, and Bergeret stood up in a circle round him. They were ignorant of his story, lost now in the immemorial past. They only knew that he had been the disciple, the friend, and the companion of Lacordaire and Montalembert, that he had opposed, as far as the precise limits of his rights and his office permitted, the establishment of the Empire, that in former days he had been subjected to the insults of Louis Veuillot,* and that he went every Sunday to mass, with a great book under his arm. Like all the town, they recognised that he retained his old-world

* Louis Veuillot, author and journalist, born 1813, and much given to duels, both with words and swords.

honesty and the glory of having maintained the cause of liberty throughout his whole life. But not one of them could have told of what type was his liberalism, for none of them had read this sentence in a pamphlet, published by M. Cassignol in 1852, on the affairs of Rome : "There is no liberty save that of the man who believes in Jesus Christ, and in the moral dignity of man." It was said that, still remaining active in mind at his age, he was classifying his correspondence and working at a book on the relations between Church and State. He still spoke fluently and brightly.

During the conversation which he followed with difficulty, on hearing a mention of the name of M. Garrand, the public prosecutor of the Republic, he remarked, looking down at the knob of his stick as though it were the solitary witness of those bygone days that still survived :

"In 1838 I knew at Lyons a public prosecutor for the Crown who had a high idea of his duties. He used to maintain that one of the attributes of public administration was infallibility, and that the king's prosecutor could no more be in the wrong than the king himself. His name was M. de Clavel, and he left some valuable works on criminal cross-examination."

Then the old man was silent, alone with his memories in the midst of men.

Paillot, on the doorstep, was watching what was going on outside.

"Here is M. Roquincourt coming out of the house."

M. Cassignol, thinking only of past events, said :

"I started at the bar. I was under the orders of M. de Clavel, who used again and again to repeat to me : 'Grasp this maxim thoroughly : The interests of the prisoner are sacred, the interests of society are doubly sacred, the interests of justice are thrice sacred.' Metaphysical principles had in those days more influence on men's minds than they have nowadays."

"That's very true," said M. de Terremondre.

"They are carrying away a bedside-table, some linen, and a little truck," said Paillot. "These are doubtless articles to be used in evidence."

M. de Terremondre, no longer able to restrain himself, went forward to watch the loading of the truck. Suddenly, knitting his brows, he exclaimed :

"Sacrebleu !"

Then, seeing Paillot's inquiring look, he added :

"It's nothing ! nothing !"

Cunning collector that he was, he had just caught sight of a water-jug in *porcelaine à la Reine* among the articles attached, and he was making up his mind to inquire about it after the trial from Surcouf, the registrar, who was an obliging man. In getting together his collections he used artifice. "One must rise to the occasion," he used to say to himself "Times are bad."

"I was nominated deputy at twenty-two years of age," resumed M. Cassignol. "At that time my long, curly hair, my beardless, ruddy cheeks, gave me a look of youth that rendered me desperate. In order to inspire respect I had to affect an air of solemnity and to wear an aspect of severity. I carried out my duties with a diligence that brought its reward. At thirty-three years of age I became attorney-general at Puy."

"It is a picturesque town," said M. Mazure.

"In the performance of my new duties I had to inquire into an affair of little interest, if one only took account of the nature of the crime and the character of the accused, but which had indeed its own importance, since it was a matter that involved the death sentence. A fairly prosperous farmer had been found murdered in his bed. I pass over the circumstances of the crime, which yet remain fixed in my memory, although they were as commonplace as possible. I need only say that, from the opening of the inquiry, suspicions fell on a ploughman, a servant of the victim. This was a man of thirty. His name was Poudrailles, Hyacinthe Poudrailles. On the day following the crime he had suddenly disappeared, and was found in a wine-shop, where

he was spending pretty freely.   Strong circum-
stantial evidence pointed to him as the author of
this murder.   A sum of sixty francs was found on
him, for the possession of which he could not
account; his clothes bore traces of blood.   Two
witnesses had seen him prowling round the farm on
the night of the crime.   It is true that another
witness swore to an alibi, but that witness was a
well-known bad character.

"The examination had been very well managed
by a judge of consummate ability.   The case for the
prosecution was drawn up with much skill.   But
Poudrailles had made no confession.   And in court,
during the whole course of the cross-examination,
he fenced himself about with a series of denials from
which nothing could dislodge him.   I had prepared
my address as public prosecutor with all the care of
which I was capable and with all the conscientious-
ness of a young man who does not wish to appear
unfitted for his high duties.   I brought to the
delivery of it all the ardour of my youth.   The
alibi furnished by the woman Cortot, who pretended
that she had kept Poudrailles in her house at Puy
during the night of the crime, was a great obstacle
to me.   I set myself to break it down.   I threatened
the woman Cortot with the penalties attaching to
perjury.   One of my arguments made a special
impression on the mind of the jury.   I reminded

them that, according to the report of the neighbours, the watch-dogs had not barked at the murderer. That was because they knew him. It was, then, no stranger. It was the ploughman; it was Poudrailles. Finally I called for the death penalty, and I got it. Poudrailles was condemned to death by a majority of votes. After the reading of the sentence, he exclaimed in a loud voice : 'I am innocent!' At this a terrible doubt seized me. I felt that, after all, he might be speaking the truth, and that I did not myself possess that certainty with which I had inspired the minds of the jury. My colleagues, my chiefs, my seniors, and even the counsel for the defence came to congratulate me on this brilliant success, to applaud my youthful and formidable eloquence. These praises were sweet to me. You know, gentlemen, Vauvenargues' dainty fancy about the first rays of glory. Yet the voice of Poudrailles saying, 'I am innocent' thundered in my ears.

"My doubts still remained with me, and I was forced again and again to go over my speech for the prosecution in my mind.

"Poudrailles' appeal was dismissed, and my un-certainty increased. At that time it was compara-tively seldom that reprieves arrested the carrying out of the death sentence. Poudrailles petitioned in vain for a commutation of the sentence. On the morning of the day fixed for the execution, when

the scaffold had already been erected at Martouret,
I went to the prison, got them to open the condemned cell to me, and alone, face to face with the
prisoner, said to him : 'Nothing can alter your fate.
If there remains in you one good feeling, in the
interests of your own soul and to set my mind at
rest, Poudrailles, tell me whether you are guilty of
the crime for which you are condemned.'   He
looked at me for some moments without replying.
I still see his dull face and wide, dumb mouth.   I
had a moment of terrible anguish.   At last he bent
his head right down and murmured in a feeble but
distinct voice : 'Now that I have no hope left, I
may as well tell you that I did it.   And I had more
trouble than you would believe, because the old
man was strong.   All the same, he was a bad lot.'
When I heard this final confession I heaved a deep
sigh of relief."

M. Cassignol stopped, gazed fixedly for a long
time at the knob of his stick with his faded, washed-
out eyes, and then uttered these words :

"During my long career as a magistrate I have
never known of a single judicial error."

"That's a reassuring statement," said M. de
Terremondre.

"It makes my blood run cold with horror,"
murmured M. Bergeret.

XVI

THAT year, as usual, M. Worms-Clavelin, the *préfet*, went shooting at Valcombe, at the house of M. Delion, an iron-master and a member of the General Council, who had the finest shooting in the district. The *préfet* enjoyed himself very much at Valcombe ; he was flattered at meeting there many people of good family, especially the Gromances and the Terremondres, and he took a deep joy in winging pheasants. Here he was to be seen pacing the woodland paths in exuberant spirits. He shot with twisted body, with raised shoulders and bent head, with one eye closed and brows knitted, in the style of the inhabitants of Bois-Colombes, the book-makers and restaurant-keepers, his original shooting companions. He proclaimed noisily, with tactless delight, the birds that he had brought down ; and by now and then attributing to himself those that had fallen to his neighbours' guns, he aroused an indignation which he immediately allayed by the placidity of his temper and by entire ignorance of

the fact that any one could possibly be vexed with
him. In all his behaviour he united pleasantly
enough the importance of an official with the familiarity of a cheerful guest. He flung their titles at
men as though they were nicknames, and because,
like all the department, he knew that M. de
Gromance was an oft-betrayed husband, at every
meeting he would give this man of ceremony several
affectionate little taps without any apparent reason.
Among the company at Valcombe he imagined
himself to be popular, and he was not entirely wrong.
When, despite his underbred manners and toadying
air, his companions had got off scot-free of both
shot and impertinences, he was considered dexterous,
and they said that, at bottom, he had tact.

This year he had succeeded better than ever in
the capitalist circle. It was known that he was
opposed to the income tax, which in private conversation he had felicitously described as inquisitorial. At
Valcombe, therefore, he was the recipient of the con-
gratulations of a grateful society, and Madame
Delion smiled on him, softening for him her steel-blue
eyes and her majestic forehead crowned with bandeaux
of iron-grey.

On leaving his room, where he had been dressing
for dinner, he saw the lissom figure of Madame
de Gromance gliding along the dark corridor, with a
rustle of clothes and jewels. In the dusk her bare

shoulders seemed barer than ever. He frisked
forward to overtake her, seized her by the waist
and kissed her on the neck. When she freed herself hurriedly, he said to her in reproachful accents :

"Why so cruel to *me*, Countess ?"

Then she gave him a box on the ears which
surprised him greatly.

On the ground-floor landing he came upon Noémi,
who, very seemly in her dress of black satin covered
with black tulle, was slowly drawing her long gloves
over her arms. He made a friendly little sign to her
with his eye. He was a good husband, and regarded
his wife with a good deal of esteem and some admiration.

She deserved it, for she had need of rare tact not
to ruffle the anti-Jewish society of Valcombe. And
she was not unpopular there. She had even won
their sympathy. And what was most astonishing,
she did not seem an outsider.

In that great cold provincial salon she assumed
an awe-stricken face and a placid demeanour which
produced a doubt of her intelligence, but proclaimed
her honest, sweet, and good. With Madame Delion
and the other women, she admired, approved, and
held her tongue. And if a man of some intelligence
and experience entered into a *tête-à-tête* with her, she
made herself still more demure, modest, and timid,
with downcast eyes ; then suddenly she hurled some

broad jest at him, which tickled him by its unexpected‚ ness, and which he regarded as a special favour, coming from so prim a mouth and so reserved a mind.   She captivated the hearts of the old sparks. Without a gesture, without a movement, without the flutter of a fan, with an imperceptible quiver of her eyelashes and a swift pursing of the lips, she insinuated ideas that flattered them.   She made a conquest of M. Mauricet himself, who, great connoisseur as he was, said of her :

" She has always been plain, she is no longer even attractive, but she is a woman."

M. Worms-Clavelin was placed at table between Madame Delion and Madame Laprat-Teulet, wife of the senator of . . .   Madame Laprat-Teulet was a sallow little woman, whom one always seemed to be looking at through gauze, so soft were her features. As a young girl, she had been steeped in religion as if it had been oil.   Now, the wife of a clever man who had married her for her fortune, she wallowed in unctuous piety, while her husband devoted his energies to the anti-clerical and secular parties.   She gave herself up to endless petty tasks.   And deeply attached as she was to her wedded condition, when a demand was lodged before the Senate for the authorisation of judicial proceedings against Laprat-Teulet and several other senators, she offered two candles in the Church of Saint-Exupère, before the painted statue of Saint Anthony, in order that by his good offices her husband's opponents might be non-suited. And it was in that way that the affair ended. A pupil of Gambetta, M. Laprat-Teulet had in his possession certain small documents, a photographic reproduction of which he had sent at a timely moment to the Keeper of the Seals. Madame Laprat-Teulet, in the zeal of her gratitude, had a marble slab put up, as a votive-offering, on the wall of the chapel, with this inscription drawn up by the venerable M. Laprune himself: *To Saint Anthony from a Christian wife, in gratitude for an unexpected blessing.* Since then M. Laprat-Teulet had retrieved his position. He had given serious pledges to the Conservatives, who hoped to utilise his great financial talents in the struggle against socialism. His political position had become satisfactory again, provided he affronted no one and did not seize the reins of power for himself.

And with her waxen fingers Madame Laprat-Teulet embroidered altar-frontals.

"Well, madame," said the *préfet* to her, after the soup, "are your good works prospering? Do you know that, after Madame Cartier de Chalmot, you are the lady in the department who presides over the largest number of charities?"

She made no answer. He recollected that she was deaf, and, turning towards Madame Delion:

"Tell me, I beg you, madame, about Saint Anthony's charity. It was this poor Madame Laprat-Teulet who made me think of it. My wife tells me it is a new cult that is becoming the rage in the department."

"Madame Worms-Clavelin is right, my dear sir. We are all devoted to Saint Anthony."

Then they heard M. Mauricet, in reply to a sentence lost in the noise, say to M. Delion :

"You flatter me, my dear sir. The Puits-du-Roi, very much neglected since Louis XIV.'s time, is not to be compared with Valcombe for its sport. There is very little game there. Still, a poacher of rare skill, named Rivoire, who honours the Puits-du-Roi with his nocturnal visits, kills plenty of pheasants there. And you've no idea what an extraordinary old blunderbuss he shoots them with. It's a specimen for a museum ! I owe him thanks for having one day allowed me to examine it at leisure. Imagine a . . ."

"I am told, madame," said the *préfet*, "that the worshippers address their requests to Saint Anthony in a sealed paper, and that they make no payment until after the blessing demanded has been received."

"Don't jest," replied Madame Delion ; "Saint Anthony grants many favours."

"It is," continued M. Mauricet, "the barrel of an old musket which has been cut through and mounted on a kind of hinge, so that it rocks up and down, and . . ."

"I thought," replied the *préfet*, "that Saint Anthony's speciality was finding lost articles."

"That is why," answered Madame Delion, "so many requests are made to him."

And she added, with a sigh :

"Who, in this world, has not lost a precious possession ?   Peace of heart, a conscience at rest, a friendship formed in childhood or . . . a husband's love ?   It is then that one prays to Saint Anthony."

"Or to his comrade," added the *préfet*, whom the ironmaster's wines had elated, and who in his innocence was confusing Saint Anthony of Padua with Saint Anthony the hermit.

"But," asked M. de Terremondre, "this Rivoire is known as the poacher to the prefecture, is he not ?"

"You are mistaken, Monsieur de Terremondre," replied the *préfet*.   "He has a still more honourable appointment as poacher to the Archbishopric.   He supplies Monseigneur's table."

"He also consents to put his skill at the service of the court," said President Peloux.

M. Delion and Madame Cartier de Chalmot were conversing together in low tones :

"My son Gustave, dear lady, is going to serve his mi͟ary term this year.   I should so much like him to be placed under General Cartier de Chalmot."

"Do not set your heart on that, monsieur. My husband hates favouritism, and he is chary of granting leave; he expects lads of good family to show an example of work. And he has imbued all his colonels with his principles."

". . . And the barrel of this musket," continued M. Mauricet, "corresponds with no recognised bore, so that Rivoire can only make use of undersized cartridges. You can easily imagine . . ."

The *préfet* was unfolding certain arguments calculated to bring Madame Delion completely over to the government, and he concluded with this noble thought :

"At the moment when the Czar is coming on a visit to France, it is necessary that the Republic should identify itself with the upper classes of the nation in order to put them in touch with our great ally, Russia."

Meanwhile, with the calm of a Madonna, Noémi was kissing feet with M. *le président* Peloux, who had been feeling about for hers under the table.

Young Gustave Delion was saying in a low voice to Madame de Gromance :

"I hope that this time you will not keep me hanging about as you did on the day when you were playing the fool with that dotard of a Mauricet, whilst

I had no other amusement in your yellow drawing-room than to potter with the works of the clock."

"What an excellent woman Madame Laprat-Teulet is!" exclaimed Madame Delion in a sudden outburst of affection.

"Excellent," said the *préfet*, swallowing a quarter of a pear. "It is a pity that she is as deaf as a post. Her husband also is an excellent man, and very intelligent. I am glad to see that people are beginning to readjust their views of him. He has gone through a difficult time. The enemies of the Republic wanted to compromise him in order to discredit the government. He has been the victim of schemes that aimed at excluding from Parliament the leading men belonging to the business world. Such an exclusion would lower the level of national representation and would be in all respects deplorable."

For a moment he remained thoughtful; then he said sadly :

"Besides, no further scandals can be hatched ; no more charges are being trumped up. And there we have one of the most grievous results of this campaign of calumny, carried on with unheard-of audacity."

"Perhaps it is as well!" sighed Madame Delion, thoughtfully and meaningly.

Then suddenly, with a burst of fervour :

"Monsieur *le préfet*, give us back our dear religious orders, let our Sisters of Charity return to the hospitals and our God to the schools whence you have expelled Him.   No longer prevent our rearing our sons as Christians and . . . we shall be very near to a mutual understanding."

Hearing these words, M. Worms-Clavelin flung up his hands, as well as his knife, on which was a morsel of cheese, and exclaimed with heartfelt sincerity : " Good God ! madame, don't you see that the streets of the county town are black with curés, and that there are monks behind all the gratings ? And as for your young Gustave, damn it ! it isn't I who prevent him from going to mass all day instead of running after the girls ! "

M. Mauricet was finishing his description of the marvellous blunderbuss, amid the clatter of voices, the echo of laughter, and the little tinkling taps of silver upon china.

M. *le préfet* Worms-Clavelin, who was in a hurry to smoke, passed out first into the billiard-room.   He was soon joined there by President Peloux, to whom he held out a cigar :

" Have one, do !   They are capital. '

And in reply to M. Peloux's thanks, showing the box of regalias, he answered :

" Don't thank me ; it is one of our host's cigars."

This joke was one of his stock ones.

At last M. Delion appeared, leading the bulk of the guests, who with greater gallantry had been chatting for a few minutes with the ladies. He was listening approvingly to M. de Gromance, who was explaining to him how necessary it was in shooting to calculate distances accurately.

"For instance," he said, "on uneven ground a hare seems relatively distant, whilst, on level ground, it seems nearer by more than fifty metres. It is on this account that . . ."

"Come," said M. *le préfet* Worms-Clavelin, taking down a cue from the rack, "come, Peloux, shall we play a game ?"

M. *le préfet* Worms-Clavelin was a pretty fair stroke at billiards ; but M. *le président* Peloux gave him points. A little Norman attorney who, at the close of a disastrous estate case, had been forced to sell his practice, he had been appointed a judge at the time when the Republic was purging the magistracy. Sent from one end of France to the other, in courts where the knowledge of the law had almost disappeared, his skill in sharp practice made him useful, and his ministerial relations secured him advancement. Yet everywhere a vague rumour of his past pursued him, and people refused to treat him with respect. But luckily he was wise enough to know how to endure persistent rebuffs. He bore affronts placidly. M. Lerond, deputy attorney-

general, now a barrister at the bar at . . ., said of
him in the Salle des Pas-Perdus : " He is a man
of intelligence who knows the distance between his
seat and the prisoner's dock." Yet that public
approval which he had not sought, and which evaded
him, had at length, by a sudden recoil, come of its
own accord. For the last two years the whole society
of the district had looked upon President Peloux as
an upright magistrate. They admired his courage
when, smiling placidly between his two pale assessors,
he had condemned to five years' imprisonment three
confederate anarchists, guilty of having distributed
in the barracks bills exhorting the nations to
fraternise.

"Twelve—four," announced M. *le président*
Peloux.

Having practised for a long time in the sleepy
restaurant of a county town in a rural canton, he
had learnt a close professional game. He raked his
balls into a little corner of the billiard-table and
brought off a series of cannons. M. *le préfet*
Worms-Clavelin played in the broad, splendid,
reckless style of the artist-cafés of Montmartre
and Clichy. And laying the failure of his rash
strokes to the charge of the table, he complained of
the hardness of the cushions.

"At la Tuilière," said M. de Terremondre, " in
my cousin Jacques' house, there is a billiard-table

with pockets, which dates from Louis XV.'s time, in a very low vaulted hall, of soft, whitewashed stone, where this inscription is still to be read : ' Gentlemen are requested not to rub their cues on the walls.' It is a request to which no one has paid any attention, for the vaulting is pitted with a number of little round holes, whose origin is accurately explained by this inscription."

M. *le président* Peloux was asked in several directions at once for details as to the affair in Queen Marguerite's house.   The murder of Madame Houssieu, which had excited all the district, was still arousing interest.   Every one knew that a crushing weight of evidence hung over a butcher's boy of nineteen, named Lecœur, whom folks used to see twice a week entering the old lady's house with his basket on his head.   It was also known that the prosecution was detaining two upholsterers' apprentices of fourteen and sixteen years of age as accomplices, and it was said that the crime had been committed in circumstances which made the story of it a particularly delicate one.

Being questioned on this point, M. *le président* Peloux lifted his round, ruddy head from the billiard-table and winked.

" The case is being tried *in camera*.   The scene of the murder has been reconstructed in its entirety.   I don't believe that there is a doubt left as to the acts

of debauchery which preceded the crime and facili-
tated the perpetration of it."

He took up his liqueur glass, swallowed a mouth-
ful of armagnac, smacked his lips, and said :

" Heavens ! what velvet ! "

And, when a circle of inquirers crowded round
him asking for details, the magistrate, in a low voice,
disclosed certain circumstances which provoked
murmurs of surprise and grunts of disgust.

" Is it possible ? " was the comment. " A woman
of eighty ! "

" The case," answered M. *le président* Peloux, " is
not unique.   You may take my word for it after my
experience as a magistrate.   And the young scamps
of the faubourgs know much more on this subject
than we do.   The crime in Queen Marguerite's
house is of a well-known, classified sort ; I might call
it a classic type.   I immediately scented it out as
senile debauchery, and I saw quite clearly that
Roquincourt, the prosecuting counsel, was following
a wrong track.   He had naturally ordered the arrest
of all the vagabonds and tramps found wandering
within a wide circumference.   Every one of them
aroused suspicions ; and what put the crowning touch
to his mistake was that one of them, Sieurin,
nicknamed Pied-d'Alouette, a regular old gaol-bird,
made a confession."

" How was that ? "

"He was bored with solitary confinement. He had been promised a pipe of canteen tobacco if he confessed. He did confess. He told them all they wanted. This Sieurin, who has been sentenced thirty-seven times for vagabondage, is incapable of killing a fly. He has never committed robbery. He is a simpleton, an inoffensive creature. At the time of the crime, the gendarmes saw him on Duroc hill making straw fountains and cork boats for the school children."

M. *le président* resumed his game.

"Ninety—forty. . . . During this time, Lecœur was telling all the girls in the Quartier des Carreaux that he had done the deed, and the keepers of disorderly houses were bringing to the police-inspector Madame Houssieu's earrings, chain, and rings that the butcher-boy had distributed among their inmates. This Lecœur, like so many other murderers, gave himself up. But Roquincourt, in a rage, left Sieurin, or Pied-d'Alouette, in solitary confinement. He is still there. Ninety-nine . . . and one hundred."

"Splendid!" said M. *le préfet* Worms-Clavelin.

"So," murmured M. Delion, "this woman of eighty-three had still . . . It is incredible!"

But Dr. Fornerol, agreeing with President Peloux's opinion, declared that the case was not as unusual as they fancied, and he supplied the physiological explanation, which was listened to with interest. Then he went on to quote different cases of sexual aberrations and wound up in these words :

" If the devil on two sticks, lifting us up in the air, were to raise the roofs of the town before our eyes, we should see appalling sights, and we should be staggered at the discovery among our fellow-citizens of so many maniacs, degenerates, mad men and mad women."

" Bah ! " said M. Worms-Clavelin, the *préfet*, " one must not look too closely into that. All these people, taken one by one, are perhaps what you say ; but together they form a superb mass of constituents and a splendid county-town population for the department."

Now, on the raised divan which overlooked the billiard-table, Senator Laprat-Teulet sat caressing his long white beard. He had the majesty of a river.

" For my part," said he, " I can only believe in goodness. Wherever I cast my eyes, I see virtue and honesty. I have been able to prove by numerous instances that the morals of the French women since the Revolution leave nothing to be desired, especially in the middle classes."

" I am not so optimistic," replied M. de Terre-mondre, " but I certainly did not suspect that Queen Marguerite's house hid such shameful mysteries behind its walls of crumbling woodwork and beneath the cobweb-curtains of its mullioned windows. I went to see Madame Houssieu several times; she seemed to me a miserly and mistrustful old woman, a little mad, yet like so many others. But, as they used to say in the time of Queen Marguerite:

> "She is under the sod.
> Her soul be with God ! *

She will no longer, by her lewdness, blot the scutcheon of good Philippe Tricouillard."

At that name a shout of merry laughter burst from their knowing faces. It was the secret joy and inward pride of the town, that emblematic shield, with its witness to the triple virtue and power that put this bourgeois ancestor of theirs on a level with the great condottiere of Bergamo. The people of . . . loved him, their lusty forebear, the contemporary of the king in the *Cent Nouvelles nouvelles*, their ancient alderman Philippe Tricouillard, about whom, to tell the truth, they knew nothing save the gift of nature to which he owed his illustrious surname.

The turn taken by the conversation led Dr. Fornerol to say that several instances had been cited of a similar anomaly, and that certain writers declare that at times this honourable monstrosity is transmitted hereditarily and becomes persistent in a family.

* " Elle est sous lame.
Dieu ait son âme ! "

Unluckily the line of the worthy Philippe had been extinct for more than two hundred years.

After this remark, M. de Terremondre, who was president of the Archæological Society, related a true anecdote.

"Our departmental archivist," said he, "the learned M. Mazure, has recently discovered in the garrets of the prefecture some documents relating to a charge of adultery, brought, at the very period when Philippe Tricouillard was flourishing, towards the end of the fifteenth century, by Jehan Tabouret against Sidoine Cloche, his wife, for the reason that the aforesaid Sidoine, having had three children at a birth, Sieur Jehan Tabouret only acknowledged two of them as his, and maintained that the third was by another man, for he averred that he was constitutionally incapable of begetting more than two at a time. And he gave a reason for this, founded on an error then common among matrons, barber-surgeons, and apothecaries, who each as eagerly as the others professed to believe that the normal frame of a man was physiologically incapable of begetting more than twins, and that all over the number of pledges which the father can produce should be disowned. For this reason, poor Sidoine was convicted by the judge of having played the harlot, and for this put naked on an ass, with her head towards the tail, and thus led through the town to the pond at Les Evés, where she was ducked three times.   She would scarcely have suffered thus if her wicked husband had been as generously gifted by Dame Nature as good Philippe Tricouillard."

XVII

N front of Rondonneau's house-door, the *préfet* glanced to right and left to see that he was not being spied upon. He had heard that it was said in the town that he went to the jeweller's house for assignations and that Madame Lacarelle had been seen following him into this house, called the House of the Two Satyrs. He felt very bad-tempered over this. He had another cause of annoyance. *Le Libéral*, which had treated him respectfully for a long time, had attacked him vigorously over the departmental budget. He was censured by the Conservative organ for having made a transfer to conceal the expenses of the electoral propaganda. M. *le préfet* Worms-Clavelin was perfectly honest. Money inspired him with respect as well as love. He felt before " Property " that feeling of religious terror that the moon inspires in dogs. With him wealth had become a cult.

His budget was very honestly put together. And, apart from the irregularities that had now become

regular as the result of a faulty administration common to the whole Republic, nothing worthy of blame
could be discovered in it.   M. Worms-Clavelin knew
this.   He felt himself strong in his integrity.   But
the polemics of the press put him out of patience.   His
heart was saddened by the animosity of his opponents
and the rancour of the parties that he believed he had
disarmed.   After so many sacrifices he was pained at
not having won the esteem of the Conservatives, which
he secretly valued far more highly than the friendship
of the Republicans.   He would have to inspire *le
Phare* with pointed and forceful replies, to conduct a
lively, and, perhaps protracted war.   This thought
was harassing to the deep slothfulness of his mind
and alarming to his prudence, which feared every
action as a source of peril.

Thus he was in a very bad temper.   And it was in
a sharp voice that, throwing himself into the old leather
arm-chair, he inquired of Rondonneau junior whether
M. Guitrel had arrived.   M. Guitrel had not yet
come.   So M. Worms-Clavelin, roughly snatching
a paper from the jeweller's desk, tried to read while
smoking his cigar.   But neither political ideas nor
tobacco-smoke served to dispel the gloomy pictures
that crowded into his mind.   He read with his eyes,
but thought of the attacks of *le Libéral :* "Transfer !
There are not fifty people in the county town who
know what a transfer is.   And here I can see all the

idiots in the department shaking their heads and solemnly repeating the phrase in their newspaper : 'We regret to see that M. *le préfet* has not abandoned the detestable and exploded practice of making transfers.' " He fell into thought. The ash from his cigar lavishly bestrewed his waistcoat. He went on thinking : " Why does *le Libéral* attack me ? I got its candidate returned. My department shows the greatest number of new adherents at election-times." He turned over the page of the paper. He thought on again : " I have not covered up a deficit. The sums voted on the presentation of the estimates have not been spent in a different way from what was proposed. These people don't know how to read a budget. And they are disingenuous." He shrugged his shoulders ; and gloomy, indifferent to the cigar ash which covered his chest and thighs, he plunged into the reading of his paper.

His eyes fell on these lines :

" We learn that a fire having broken out in a faubourg of Tobolsk, sixty wooden houses have fallen a prey to the flames. In consequence of the disaster more than a hundred families are homeless and starving."

As he read this, M. *le préfet* Worms-Clavelin emitted a deep shout, something like a triumphal growl, and, aiming a kick at the jeweller's desk :

" I say, Rondonneau, Tobolsk is a Russian town, isn't it ? "

Rondonneau, raising his innocent, bald head towards the *préfet*, replied that Tobolsk was, indeed, a town in Asiatic Russia.

" Well," cried M. *le préfet* Worms-Clavelin, " we are going to give an entertainment for the benefit of the sufferers by the fire at Tobolsk."

And he added between his teeth :

" I'll make . . . a Russian entertainment for 'em. I shall have six weeks' peace, and they won't talk any more about transfers."

At that moment Abbé Guitrel, with anxious eyes, his hat under his arm, entered the jeweller's shop.

" Do you know, monsieur l'abbé," said the *préfet* to him, " that, by general request, I am authorising entertainments for the benefit of the sufferers from the fire at Tobolsk—concerts, special performances, bazaars, &c. ? I hope that the Church will join in these benevolent entertainments."

" The Church, monsieur *le préfet*," replied Abbé Guitrel, " has her hands full of comfort for the afflicted who come to her. And doubtless her prayers . . ."

" *À propos*, my dear abbé, your affairs are not getting on at all. I come from Paris. I saw the friends whom I have at the Department of Religion.

And I bring back bad news. To start with, there
are eighteen of you."

"Eighteen ?"

"Eighteen candidates for the bishopric of Tourcoing. In the first rank is Abbé Olivet, curé of one
of the richest parishes in Paris, and the president's
candidate. Next there is Abbé Lavardin, vicar-
general at Grenoble. Ostensibly, he is supported
by the nuncio."

"I have not the honour of knowing M. Lavardin,
but I do not think he can be the candidate of the
nunciature. It is possible that the nuncio has his
favourite. But assuredly that favourite remains
unknown. The nunciature does not solicit on
behalf of its protégés. It insists on their appointment."

"Ah ! ah ! monsieur l'abbé, they are cute at the
nunciature."

"Monsieur *le préfet*, the members of it are not all
eminent in themselves ; but they have on their side
unbroken tradition, and their action is guided by
secular rules. It is a force, monsieur *le préfet*, a
great force."

"By Jove, yes ! But we were saying that there
is the president's candidate and the nuncio's candidate. There is also your own Archbishop's candidate. When they first mentioned him, I thought
to myself that it was you. . . . We were wrong,

my poor friend. Monseigneur Charlot's protégé—
I'll wager you won't guess who it is."

"Don't make a wager, monsieur *le préfet*, don't
make a wager. I would bet that the candidate of
Monseigneur the Cardinal-Archbishop is his vicar-
general, M. de Goulet."

"How do you know that? I did not know it
myself."

"Monsieur *le préfet*, you are not unaware that
Monseigneur Charlot dreads that he may find himself saddled with a coadjutor, and that his old age,
otherwise so august and serene, is darkened by this
fear. He is afraid lest M. de Goulet should, so to
say, attract this nomination to himself, as much by
his personal merits as by the knowledge that he has
acquired of the affairs of the diocese. And His
Eminence is still more desirous, and even impatient,
to separate himself from his vicar-general, since
M. de Goulet belongs by birth to the nobility of
the district, and through that fact shines with a
brilliancy which is far too dazzling for Monseigneur
Charlot. Since, on the contrary, Monseigneur does
not rejoice in being the son of an honest artisan who,
like Saint Paul, worked at the trade of weaver !"

"You know, Monsieur Guitrel, that they also talk
of M. Lantaigne. He is the protégé of Madame
Cartier de Chalmot. And General Cartier de Chalmot, although clerical and reactionary, is much

respected in Paris. He is recognised as one of the ablest and most intelligent of our generals. Even his opinions, at this moment, are advantageous rather than harmful to him. With a ministry disposed to reunion, reactionaries get all that they want. They are needed ; they give the turn to the scale. And then the Russian alliance and the Czar's friendship have contributed to restore to the aristocracy and the army of our nation a part of their ancient prestige. We are shunting the Republic on to a certain distinction of mind and manners. Moreover, a general tendency towards authority and stability is declaring itself. I do not, however, believe that M. Lantaigne has great chances. In the first place, I have reported most unfavourably with regard to him. I have represented him in high places as a militant monarchist. I have described his uncompromising ways, his cross-grained temperament. And I have painted a sympathetic portrait of you, my dear Guitrel. I have shown off your moderation, your pliancy, your politic mind, your respect for republican institutions."

"I am very grateful to you for your kindness, monsieur *le préfet*. And what did they reply ?"

"You want to know that. Well! they replied : 'We know such candidates as your M. Guitrel. Once nominated, they are worse than the others. They show more zeal against us. That is easily

accounted for.   They have more to beg pardon **for**
of their own party.' "

" Is it possible, monsieur *le préfet*, that they talked
like this in high places ? "

" Ha ! yes.   And my interlocutor added this :
' I do not like candidates for the episcopacy who
show too much zeal for our institutions.   If I
could get a hearing, the choice would be made
from among the others.   In the civil and political
ranks they prefer officials who are most devoted,
most attached to the government.   Nothing can be
better.   But there are no priests devoted to the
Republic.   In this case, the wise thing is always
to take the most honest men.' "

And the *préfet*, throwing the chewed end of his
cigar into the middle of the floor, finished with
these words :

" You see, my poor Guitrel, that your affairs are
not making headway."

M. Guitrel stammered :

" I do not see, Monsieur *le préfet*, I do not perceive anything, in such speeches, that is calculated
to produce in you this impression of . . . dis-
couragement.   On the contrary, I should rather
derive from it a sentiment of . . . confidence. . . ."

M. *le préfet* Worms-Clavelin lit a cigar and said
with a laugh :

" Who knows whether they are not right, at the

bureaux ? . . . But reassure yourself, my dear abbé, I do not abandon you. Let's see, whom have we on our side ? "

He opened his left hand, in order to count on his fingers.

They both considered.

They found a senator of the department who was beginning to emerge from the difficulties into which the recent scandals had plunged him, a retired general, politician, publicist and financier, the bishop of Ecbatana, well known in the artistic world, and Théophile Mayer, the friend of the ministers.

"But, my dear Guitrel," cried the *préfet*, "you have only the rag-tag and bobtail on your side."

Abbé Guitrel endured these manners, but he did not like them. He looked at the *préfet* with a saddened air and pressed his sinuous lips together. M. Worms-Clavelin, who had no spite, regretted the playfulness of his words and took pains to console the old man :

"Come ! come ! they are by no means the worst protectors. Besides, my wife is for you. And Noémi by herself is well able to make a bishop."